AF661455

Black, White and Polka Dot

Black, White and Polka Dot

Aparna Jha

Manas Publications
New Delhi-110 002 (INDIA)

MANAS PUBLICATIONS
(Publishers, Distributors, Importers & Exporters)
4858, Prahlad Street,
24, Ansari Road, Darya Ganj,
New Delhi - 110 002 (INDIA)
Ph.: 23260783, 23265523 (O); 27131660, 27143052 (R)
Fax: 011-23272766
E-mail: manaspublications@vsnl.com

© Aparna Jha

First Published 2003

ISBN 81-7049-173-8

No part of this publication can be reproduced, photocopied, translated, etc., in any form whatsoever, without prior written permission of the publisher.

The views expressed in this book are those of the author and not necessarily of the publisher. The publisher is not responsible for the views of the author and authenticity of the data, in any way whatsoever.

Typeset at
Manas Publications

Printed in India at
Shree Balaji Arts
and Published by Mrs Suman Lata for
Manas Publications, 4858, Prahlad Street,
24, Ansari Road, Darya Ganj,
New Delhi - 110 002 (INDIA)

For Braj, my husband.

Preface

It is interesting how I started writing. My maid, who worked with me full-time, had left. She had looked after our daughter, while I was away working with a solicitors firm, in an upmarket place in the capital. Since the baby was small, I had to stay back. My husband suggested I utilize free time by learning to operate the computer. So I started keying in the words that came to my mind. He seemed to like my writings in the beginning, and suggested, I should write short stories. When the baby slept, I wrote. At times the urge to write would be so strong I would wait for the baby to sleep so that I could sit on the PC and start writing. The whole experience was exhilarating. I wanted to write and write more, it became some sort of an obsession.

And then it became an addiction. When I would start with a story, I would be in a hurry to complete it. I would forget food, everything. And then I would coax Braj, my husband, to read it. In the beginning he showed interest, some appreciation, but soon it changed. He said he did not want to read them, I would persist. I coaxed, I cajoled, and finally, I threatened him.

My parents also read a few of them. My father got them photocopied when I went to visit them; I elicited a promise from my mother that she would read them, when at leisure.

'Let me come back after seeing two-three patients', she would promise, 'then I will read all your stories.' I doubt if she read my stories.

In the beginning I had some encouragement. Write, it is a good pastime. Get over your Elizabethan hangover. You will certainly write better. Let there be some more touch of emotions. Make it more dramatic.

And then the discouragement. You see, I was told, you should devote more time to your profession. I was a lawyer, I was reminded, and I should remain one. I was simply wasting my time.

I continued writing. One story after another. Some I would like, some I would discard.

I have drawn heavily from my experience as a lawyer, a woman, and above all, a mother. Childhood experiences, lives of neighbours, the domestic help, who had been with us for years, all this have been a good story material. I wrote these stories over a period of two-three years. When I started writing, I was a junior. Legal profession can be taxing, and with a small child clamouring for attention, I had to find time to write.

I do not know how will these stories be received. But I have loved writing each one of them. In fact, I remember laughing after almost every paragraph I wrote in 'The Family Disappears.' 'Rain and Thunder' brought a lump to my throat.

Acknowledgments

My parents for making me what I am.

Gopu you have always been there.

Lola I hope you like it when you grow up.

Phunnu *Bhaiyya* thank you for having faith in me.

Padma *Masi* my mother says I write like you.

Contents

Mohini Came Back

It did happen once or twice a year but this time things got quite out of hand. The child was also growing up, he could understand a thing or two and started wailing and saying '*Ma, ma,*' with his tiny hands, the size of a paper weight they kept on their study table, outstretched, entreating the two persons he trusted most, to stop making him terrified. Who listens to a child when in fury, the revengeful mind gets more and more spiteful. The child was tossed in a corner, his eyes very frightened.

It was Kuntal and Mohini. The latter, her breath unsteady with anger, bared her teeth and bit into Kuntal's flesh with all the might she could gather. Kuntal howled. He hit her hard on her back, her hands, her thighs, his eyes furious. Mohini hurled him off the bed with full force, he tried to climb back. He was again pushed back, his head was hit by the corner of the bed, he shut his eyes tight. 'I'll kill you,' Kuntal was hissing. He caught hold of her and started showering blows on her. Such excruciating pain. More than that, the humiliation. 'You savage!' Kuntal spat, ' the whole lot is a pack of savages.' By now Mohini had reached the door; she said she was leaving him. Kuntal knew Mohini.

When angry, she lost control over her senses, she could have done just anything, throttled herself, left the house and drowned herself in a ditch, got crushed under a bus. Kuntal did not want any such thing to happen.

But Mohini had gone mad. Cheenu, their son, took his mother's side. 'Mamma's tail,' Kuntal joked when Cheenu snuggled close to his mother, holding the black and blue *dupatta* his mother had bought when she had gone to the shop to buy him some T-shirts. There was something in the way the colours black and blue had been harmonized that compelled his mother to go for it, despite the fact that at that time she did not have a *salwar suit* on which she could wear that.

Cheenu was tugging at the same black and blue *dupatta* while Mohini was using full force to pull open the door, trying to get past Kuntal. Kuntal stood in her way. '*Saubhagyavati Mohini*', her father-in-law wrote when he referred to her in his letters. 'Baby faced Mohini', Kuntal would say fondly, his hands on her body, his face taut with passion.

Cheenu was wailing. He was calling his mother. Kuntal ran, opened the wooden drawer with one of the knobs missing, and pulled out Cheenu's sneakers. He stuffed Cheenu's tiny feet into those shoes and hissed, 'Go, go with your mother.'

Mohini ran downstairs, her faculties numb with anger, and holding the tiny fingers of her son, she pulled him along with her. Normally she would have gone to a nearby park or would have walked and walked till her anger had been spent and come back exhausted. Today it was different. She walked past Sharma uncle.

'Cheenu *baba*, where are you going with your mother?' Cheenu looked at his mother who in turn looked at Sharma uncle and said, 'Actually, Cheenu wanted to go for a walk,' she looked at Cheenu, half frightened he would reveal the truth. 'If he says he has to go, he has to go.' Cheenu was silent. 'Cheenu, do *namaste*,' Mohini tried folding her son's hands, her own hands shaking, only she knew how difficult it was to put up this pretence.

Mohini thought of something and she turned back. 'Cheenu, will you stay here while I go and get my purse from upstairs?' Cheenu nodded. Mohini left him near the staircase, the rectangular, wooden letter-boxes with the flat numbers written neatly on them, above his head. 'And don't touch that,' Mohini pointed towards the meters.

She ran upstairs. She pulled open the iron gate, left ajar by their maid, one who looked after Cheenu when they went to their place of work, one who was standing there, not knowing how to react. Mohini tore past her, her face red as brick. She pulled open the cupboard, took her tiny purse and ran back. Cheenu, she saw, was standing in the same place she had left him. She held his tiny fingers, and walked past the park, the big gate, and reached the *rickshaw-wallah*.

'Mother Dairy'', she whispered, afraid her voice would give her away. She hated to show her emotions in public.

'Ten', the *rickshaw-wallah* said nonchalantly, taking a calculated risk.

'No', Mohini was firm, 'we pay only seven rupees for that distance.'

He motioned towards the seat, its black leather torn and stitched at several places. Mohini hauled Cheenu on it, who sat on the *rickshaw* with his feet dangling.

'*Ma*, I will hold your dress for you,' Cheenu offered, his mother's *kurta*, a pale green, was swaying, 'you hold your purse.' Mohini felt a fresh pang of pain. She felt like crying. She kissed Cheenu on his hair.

They were soon at Mother Dairy, but Mohini did not know where to get the bus from. Though she used to frequent this place earlier, she had problem in concentrating. '*Ma*, ask somebody', Cheenu suggested, the sheer volume of traffic filled him with dread; he clung to his mother who had hauled him on to her lap, his warm face with its smooth breathing, filling her with a sense of security.

They were on the whiteline bus which would take them to *Palika Bazaar*, the centrally air conditioned market in the heart of Delhi, at a flat rate of ten rupees per passenger. Earlier it was five, then they increased it to seven, and now it is ten. They won't charge Cheenu, she calculated, finances always gave her a headache, though Kuntal alleged she took abnormal interest in finances. 'How much have we earned this month?' For her, Kuntal said, this was of immeasurable interest.

'Railway Station! Railway Station!'

Cheenu panicked. '*Ma*, where are we going? Why is uncle saying Railway Station! Railway Station!'

'I want to sleep', he pleaded, the moving bus making him drowsy. '*Ma*, let's go home,' he said. Mohini took him carefully on her lap, started patting him on his shoulders. Cheenu lay quietly.

Mohini woke up Cheenu when she thought they had reached *Palika.* 'Get down here itself', the conductor said, '*Palika , Palika*', he shouted.

'*Ma,* let's go back,' Cheenu said. Mohini ignored him, readjusting the strap of her purse which had slithered down, her face showing no emotions.

Cheenu had an ice cream, Mohini a cup of tea. A small boy, Cheenu's age but much shorter and with a mature face, was selling candy-floss. '*Hawa mithai,*' she called it when she was Cheenu's age. They ran after the vendor. He came normally in the afternoons when the womenfolk were all asleep, and he came with all the pink *hawa ka mithais* wrapped around the bamboo stick which he held aloft like the Indian flag. Mohini remembered running after him for a long time after which she lost interest and came back to play with dolls in her house with her cousins.

The tea was heavily sugared, Mohini curled her fingers around the disposable plastic glass to warm herself. They sat on the park above the *bazaar,* nothing looked unusual, many couples with children could be seen enjoying the warm winter sun. Some children were running about, Cheenu also ran. Mohini had some *bhelpooris.* Hot and spicy. She took out her handkerchief to blow her nose, patterned after her father's, in fact she resembled him in more ways than one. She bought a bottle of mineral water. She normally carried water bottle when they travelled with Cheenu, though today she didn't.

'*Ma,* call up papa,' Cheenu said. 'I don't want to go home,' Mohini said. 'I'll ask papa to come, you can go with him.'

Cheenu was sobbing. 'I can't go without you. I don't like it when you are not there.' Mohini looked at her son. She had been told many a time she did not fulfill her maternal obligations properly. Yet, the child loved her. Mohini knew. Mohini had not carried her mobile with her. She looked at the mineral water-*wallah* and called him out, '*Bhaiyya, Bhaiyya*.' The child joined her, '*Bhaiyya, Bhaiyya*.'

He did not hear them.

'I don't want to go home. Ask papa to take you along with himself.'

The child started crying. *Huaaaaaaaa*. The couples sitting in the park looked at them. Mohini was not bothered. They did not know her.

Fists and blows, she remembered, and her resolve not to go home got stronger. She had also hit Kuntal but not with such vengeance. The telephone booth was just across the road. Cheenu walked with care, his brown curls gleaming with oil, his inflated shoes making a funny *chee chee chee* as he wobbled along with his mother, the latter looked surprisingly young for her age. There were one or two of them in queue before her. Mohini sat Cheenu on the counter. He wanted to buy chewing gum for himself. Mohini obliged. So long as he did not bother her, she did not mind. It seemed Kuntal was waiting for her call.

'Where are you?' there was a note of urgency in his voice.

'On top of the underground market. *Palika Bazaar*.'

'I am coming.'

Mohini quietly replaced the telephone on the receiver and unzipped her small purse to make the payment, the credit cards peeping out. The purse was a smart one, presented to her by Kuntal on her birthday.

They went back. Mohini could see Kuntal's half sleeve sweater, the colour that you can not help looking at twice, indigo blue. She looked the other way. Kuntal extended his hands towards Cheenu who ran to his father.

'I'll take a walk,' Mohini said, both her hands joined behind her, the kind of style males adopted while walking. Kuntal always said she had more masculine traits than feminine. 'We'll come along with you,' Kuntal slipped close to her, 'the traffic police took one thousand rupees from me for over-speeding.' Mohini knew the speed, in this case, was not for thrill. She could discern his voice was laced with concern. Kuntal took Cheenu for an ice cream. Another one. Mohini refused to go with them. 'You go. I will follow you.' Cheenu was again tearful. '*Ma*, I will not go without you.'

'Say sorry, papa,' his eyes were pleading, 'let us take *Ma* back.'

Kuntal was more than ready to say sorry.

They drove quietly. Cheenu was in the back seat, his legs spread out, he was exhausted with tiredness. He fell into a gentle sleep. Mohini asked Kuntal to stop the car. 'Let me get down here, I shall take a bus back home.' It was dark and Cheenu was only half asleep. He immediately got up and wailed, '*Ma*, stay with me.'

Cheenu refused to go off to sleep after that. 'No', he said, 'You will leave me and go if I sleep.'

They did not go upstairs to their flat. Mohini did not want to. She was still angry. She still needed time to get normal.

They went to the park instead. Cheenu got up, wore his tiny shoes himself, and then extended his tiny hands towards his mother. Kuntal sat in the car for some time. He knew his wife had still not cooled down and he did not trust her. His hands on the wheels, he stared at their shadows. Mohini saw their maid looking at them from the main balcony, and asked her to get some milk for Cheenu in the park itself. Poor child had not eaten properly for a long time. Though Mohini had also not eaten proper food since morning.

Normally their maid cooked *dal* and vegetables, in the morning itself, and when Kuntal and she came back from their workplace in the evening, she boiled some rice to go with it or rolled out *rotis,* as and when asked for.

Today they were back from the office in the afternoon itself. She had come back quite hungry. They had done a lot of running around and unlike her husband, Mohini could not control her hunger for a long time. 'Hurry up, heat the food and prepare rice,' Mohini had shouted from their bedroom, its door was half shut.

'*Aaachhaaa,*' the maid had replied. Despite having stayed with them for several years, she still had the same bucolic style of talking. But she was quite useful nonetheless.

And then all this happened.

It was almost eight o'clock. The moon, Mohini felt, wore a weird expression. And she had lost all her appetite.

There is a particular pattern. If you do not eat for a long time, the sharp hunger pangs get dulled and then you do not feel like eating at all. Though Mohini was no sage she fervently desired she was one. At times she felt like quitting everything and to go to an unknown place. Where no one knew her. Where she could lose herself in anonymity. But she couldn't leave her Cheenu. Like the legendary demon whose life lay in a parrot, she knew her life depended on her son.

It was getting late and Mohini was weary. The day had been long and tiresome. She sat on the child's slide, a metallic sloping thing on which Cheenu played. The metal had a big hole at the base, at the point where the children had to stop and get off the slide and at times, Mohini feared, it was dangerous to leave the children alone there. So what she did was that she put her foot on the hole so that Cheenu, when he dropped down from above at her feet, *zoooooooooo*, there was no accident. The maid came with the glass of milk. In fact, she had fetched milk in a sipper, a pink glass made of plastic, which was broad at the top and tapered at the bottom. It had a pipe attached to it. Cheenu loved sipping his milk, laced with Bournvita.

Mohini was sad. She desperately wanted to unburden herself. She clung to Cheenu. The child touched his mother's hair, her face, his tiny finger tracing her forehead, her nose and then her chin. A tiny teardrop fell on his small finger. He said nothing. Cheenu started sipping his milk, making small bubbles as milk drained into Cheenu's mouth. The air was getting chilly, the park was getting darker. Kuntal looked from the balcony now and then.

Mohini came back, Cheenu on her lap. Mohini walked up the stairs, breathing heavily, now Cheenu weighed fifteen kilograms. She looked briefly at the marble nameplate they had hung proudly outside their house, their names written on it. She placed Cheenu gently on the bed, he took a turn, she pulled out his shoes and socks. Cheenu said something in his dream. A soft quilt hugged his body.

Then she lay beside Cheenu, hid her face in his quilt, and held him tightly. And then she let out a sob, low and smothered.

Kuntal was not there. He had gone to buy cigarettes.

Rain And Thunder

Fear. It is a strong word. It shakes you, it shatters you and it terrifies you. It is a strong feeling, like cough and cold, you have to feel it, experience it, the old man thought, sitting in his room, huddled in a corner, his eyeballs dilating every time it thundered. The flashes of lightning, the clap of thunder, all this gave him a strange feeling. He could hear sheets of rain fall on the asbestos sheet above him- *put put put put.* His umbrella needed repairing, he knew, he would remember to go to the bank the next day to withdraw some money to buy a new one. His memory was failing, he was an old and infirm man; the man for whom his past was like an old toy long discarded. Except when it thundered and poured. For that would bring back memories of his family. For he really had all of them.

His wife. She swept and mopped and cooked and cleaned; an uncomplaining woman, the old man can still see her, her glass bangles tinkling, the cotton *saree* that she draped around herself carelessly giving her a majestic look. She was his queen. And they were content with living in their two-room house with a leaking asbestos roof. During festivals like *Holi,* the old man's wife prepared special dishes; dry fruits were arranged on the table, along with the other things his wife had prepared all day long.

Anyone who came to their house on *Holi* played with colours- green, red, yellow, all kept neatly on a plate by her. Then she would offer her preparations.

The old man loved his family. Festivals were the days to celebrate. Now, of course, he dreads the approach of *Holi* or *Diwali.*

But Lalita, his daughter, was his favourite. Every morning she would insist upon sitting with the old man and eat with him, *chuda* with *dahi,* they would munch it for some time, long after sunrise. They would then go to the dairy to buy milk. Then Lalita would dress up to go to the school across the road while the old man would take his umbrella and make preparations to reach his office. Dot at ten o'clock. And then he would leave it dot at five o'clock. He would be in a hurry to reach home. For he was a family man. He certainly had a weakness for *paan,* he admitted, but he had no other vice, and he was devoted to his wife and children.

One day Lalita went to her school; she did not come back. It thundered. *Indra,* the rain God, was furious, the old man did not know why. Deeply religious, he repeated- *'Agastasye, Pulastasye Vaisantya Painava cha..'* several times. There was no reprieve. Lalita had been struck by lightning in the corridor. He stared at her corpse. Involuntarily, he extended his hands and helped Lalita sit on his lap. One last time.

Lalita, his child. He felt a lump rise in his throat. He remembered how he cried when he held her tiny fingers and took her to the school for the first time. He went to his office after that but could not concentrate. The peon had fetched tea for him that he drank in one gulp, not realizing how hot it was. While working, he fumbled at many places. He moaned. A flash of lightning. The old man got up to change the jute bag soaked by the leaking roof. It rained hard. Lalita kept coming back to him. She would have been fifteen years by now. They would have married her off.

But life went on. Lalita's absence notwithstanding. The old man got a photograph of hers- smiling, with a bouquet of flowers in her hands- and hung it in his room. A garland adorned it. The old man drew solace from looking at it every day in the morning.

Life could have been easier for him, the old man felt, had his friends Chowdhary and Sinha not gone to live with their sons on retirement. They had lived together in the same locality for more than two decades; they went for morning walk together, the old man wobbling on his walking stick- he had this problem in his right leg which, even after diagnosis and proper medication, could not be treated. They left the old man just as the others had. He had been closer to Sinha, a hirsute man with a sharp nose and eyes that kept blinking at regular intervals. All three of them would sit in the park for hours, they had nothing else to do.

It was raining hard. The old man opened the door. A woman stood at the door, and a dog. They were soaked in water. They obviously needed shelter which the old man provided. At least he would not be alone in this stormy night, he thought. He opened the rusted trunk and took out his late wife's *saree*, shiny and colourful.

The woman changed briskly and admired herself in the little mirror that was nailed to the wall. The dog barked. The old man wiped the dog dry. Now they were three of them in the room, the old man, the woman and the dog.

When the old man spoke, the dog listened. He cried with the old man when Lalita or her mother or her brothers were mentioned. The dog shared the old man's grief. He also shared the woman's grief when she told him how her husband died. The dog also felt like saying so many things, and he barked.

Put Put Put Put. O God, the old man muttered, when will this stop? Water fell in sheets. The road was empty, none dared to go out in the storm at this hour. Those who defied Nature were humbled. The old man could not sleep. The thought of the black night kept coming back to him.

On that fateful night, the old man had come back on his bicycle, old but reliable. There was a big bloody mess. Good-bye Papa! They looked at him. It had rained and thundered, he remembered. He was frightened. Very frightened. His eyeballs dilated in fear and he sat in the corner, guarding the corpses zealously. Once he got up and covered the bodies with a blanket. It was getting cold.

The woman snored. She reminded him of his own wife. She roared like a lioness when she slept. Why did not the lioness tear and eat them up that day? Instead, they tore her and his world.

The old man led a lonely existence. When alone, he thought of his past. It also became infrequent with the passage of time.

The woman and the dog slept. Everything was now much more cheerful. So different from the previous night, black as coal.

In the morning, the rain had stopped. The trees looked freshly bathed, clean and sparking. He could feel the warmth of sun on his cheeks. The old man went to the toilet. He returned and saw the woman admiring herself in the mirror. He told her she could keep the *saree*. She was happy. She walked away. And so did the dog.

The Family Disappears

At that time the only kind of families they normally had were the joint families. She had three sons, one of whom died, came under a train. She had a daughter, in fact, two, again one daughter died as she suffered from some disease I do not remember. All her sons and daughters were born to her after they migrated to Patna. Patna, the central place, where all of them flocked, came pouring in from villages, near and far, like a mad rush of water during floods. They all came from different villages, saw city life for the first time, got fascinated by it, and then decided to go back to their villages only during the summer and *dussehra* vacations. They would go nostalgic and remember the house they were born in, the exact location, the pond in which they bathed, the local school they went to, the school master with the stick fresh in mind. And after a few days, they would be desperate to go back.

So it was in Patna where all the children were born, in the government accommodation built by the *gora sahibs* for their subordinates who would assist them in administration. Once a year, the father, *Babu*, would go to the village, bring large sacks of rice, the coarse variety, black grams and lentils, *chuda*, something they fried and had with onion in the evenings, and with this *Babu* would be back within a week. They had a number of rooms in their *sarkari* accommodation, unlike the flats of today, the pigeon holes, and *Babu's* wife, *Mai,* kept aside a room which served as some sort of a granary. All this would last them a year. As to all the other expenses, *Babu's* salary took care.

All the five children were educated, even the girls.

Pandit Vivekanand came to their house once in a while. *Mai* asked him to sit on the *peedhi,* the rectangular, wooden thing, shined and polished. She reverentially served him rice which she piled in one corner, on a plate, with a lot of *ghee,* placing the bowls, pickles, and *papad* in the other corner. Then *Mai* would ask Pandit Vivekanand—the man who wore a surprisingly clean *dhoti,* oiled his hair everyday and wore *kharaun,* the wooden slippers—about her children.

It was Pandit Vivekanand who told *Mai* about Chunnu. He was her eldest son, the bright one, one who always made his mother proud of the fact that he was born to her. Chunnu she had nurtured with care, he made her bosom swell with pride, Chunnu, she now knew, will not live long. *Mai* could not sleep at night, he floated before her, her eyes were moist, she wiped the tears in the pillow cover. *Babu* was angry when he heard all this.

'Let that *Pandit* come near my house and see if I don't break his legs!'

But she was frightened. The words of *Pandit* rang in her ears. Chunnu, he told, will be crushed under a train. If he survives, he will be a big man. *Mai* did not want her son to be a big man, she simply wanted him to live.

Their quarters were near the railway station, every time the train came whistling by, Chunnu said he had to go. *Babu* said he had lost his head, they should see a doctor, *Mai* said, no. They had to propitiate the gods. She would lock all the doors before they went off to sleep. No one knows how Chunnu managed to escape. In the morning, she panicked when she saw his bed was empty, she ran to the railway station, Chunnu's body she found there. Cut into two by the train, *Mai* did not know what to do with his body. *Mai* sat there, looking at Chunnu, his thighs severed, his eyes open.

It took quite some time before she recovered from the shock. The children were neglected, the daughters took charge of the household. *Mai* says her elder daughter, Savitri, was the fair one. God took away the bright and the fair one. Savitri was married, and the news of her death reached *Mai*.

All the remaining children were married off one by one. In turn, they had their own children. *Mai's* younger daughter, Suchitra was married to a man who lived in a village.

'Today we are going to see a bride who will come with her head exposed,' the women of the village said, a girl from the city, one who must have her modern ways.

Mai grew old. She wished to have a house built on the banks of *Ganga,* the holy river, where she would go every day in the morning to take her bath. *Babu* got the house constructed wherever *Mai* wished. It was a white rectangular building, with a big courtyard in centre, and rooms on all the four sides. The *pubaria* and the *pachbaria ghar,* the rooms were named according to the direction they faced. There was a verandah, with a large wooden table, and chairs with long bars, where the children studied in the evenings under the dim light of kerosene lamps they had those days. Though electricity had reached many houses, somehow they did not get a proper electricity connection for a long time. It was, therefore, a great occasion when those electricians came to their house, wired the house, those small bulbs that emitted light, yellow in colour, were fitted, and the whole house shone.

Sharda, *Mai's* younger daughter-in-law, one who had studied in a convent school run by the missionaries, had been a good student when in school. When she was getting married, at the tender age of thirteen, the Sisters were angry. It was a case of child marriage. She can no longer study in the school, they were absolutely forthright, it is against our policies.

Sharda left the school, took her board exams from a government school and then she decided she had to study in Science College, the co-educational institution where they all went before preparing for engineering or medical entrance tests. Punnu, *Mai's* elder son, one who had married the daughter of a *zamindar*, the *zamindar* of Dularpur, somehow did not like the idea. The *bahu* of the house going to study in a co-educational institution! No, Tunnu, he was telling his younger brother, ask your wife to study in Magadh Mahila. We can never allow this. Sharda was adamant, she was not studying anywhere else. Science College was the one for her. The matter was brought up before *Babu*.

'What does the student want?' *Babu,* the patriarch of the house, was asking.

Sharda stood at the other side of the door, covering her head, and taking care that she did not show her face to either her father-in–law or her brother-in-law, something she was not supposed to do as the *bahu* of the house. *Babu* went with her. Sharda studied in Science College, something she had wanted all along.

At times the two brothers, Punnu and Tunnu, fought, and it was all very amusing to see that. Both were short tempered, had a very loud voice, and inspite of *Mai's* intervention, they quarrelled with great zeal. The entire *mohalla* they lived in was filled with their voices. They were not abusive, they simply shouted, one tried to out shout the other, while the wives and the children simply listened. All the children would be very quiet while all this lasted, and after it was all over, they would resume their work as if nothing had happened. The brothers were friends again, they would discuss things like the house tax that had to be paid, the drain which had become choked, and needed to be cleaned, the soaring prices of the vegetables. Both the wives, while cooking for their family, would defend their husbands. They made *rotis* in vast quantities, a panful of vegetables was prepared which they all had together. The children were not bothered. They were used to all this and would go to their friends to play as if nothing had happened.

Once Tunnu, who had set up a small workshop, where he intended to manufacture small spare parts, lifted a *chowki* from the house and said he needed that at his workshop. Punnu was informed about this, one of the children went and gave a faithful account of the manner in which Rambilas, the man who worked at the workshop, came with a handcart, which he parked with great difficulty in the narrow lane they lived in, and with the help of the cartpuller, he lifted the *chowki.* Punnu flew into a rage, holding his *lungi* with one hand, his slippers, made of rubber, making a flopping sound as he hurried out of his bedroom. He shouted,

'Tunnu, you *chathi ka raja,* how could you dare to remove that *chowki?'*

Undeterred by Punnu's shouting, Tunnu, an equal match, let out a deep breath and jumped out of his bed, meeting Punnu near the courtyard. Holding the clothesline where the former hung his underclothes he himself had washed, and looking at Punnu straight in his eyes, he shouted,

'That *chowki* about which you are shouting was bought by *Babu* and both of us have an equal share in it!'

'Precisely, that is why you should have consulted me before asking Rambilas to carry it away in that cart!' Now Punnu was also holding the clothesline, Tunnu's towel, the one he had washed half an hour back and which was hanging near Punnu's underclothes, brushing his face.

I do not remember who emerged victorious but it can be said with certainty that both fought for some time, after which their mother, her hair shining with the mustard oil she had rubbed in it, and which smelled badly, came running and brought about a truce.

Mai was very social, she believed in living above her station, and mingling with those she thought were important. Though she herself was the daughter of a *zamindar,* gone was the *zamindari* and its attendant luxuries. *Babu* didn't earn much and it was quite a difficult job when she was needed to mix among her rich friends who almost always gave her a complex.

And then the two brothers fought. *Mai* was a practical lady, believed in worshipping the rising sun, and had some of her favourites in the family. She believed that Tina, Tunnu's daughter, needed protection, given the fact that her mother was preparing for the medical entrance test, and her brother and she were in her care. So it was Tina's duty, when *Mai's* friends came, to entertain them, and *Mai* would instruct Tina to recite the poems she had learnt in school and off Tina would go,

'Twinkle twinkle little star

How I wonder what you are'

Neither the grandmother nor her friends would understand what all this meant, their knowledge of English being zero. But the very fact that Tina won a first prize -a glass made of plastic which she immediately filled with water and drank from- for reciting this rhyme in school, was enough to make *Mai* proud of her.

They had *kirtan* at their home, once a month, when they all sang in praise of God. *Mai* invited neighbours and the others, and she, along with Godavari, her elder daughter-in-law, cleaned and scrubbed the floor vigorously, emptied the *pachbaria ghar*, the room where the *kirtan* was held, make garlands of marigold, and cut fruits which they would then distribute as *prasad* once the *puja* was over. Tina was, at times, cajoled to sit there and sing devotional songs along with the others.

'What a religious child!' *Mai's* friends would remark, while Tina sat there and sang the *bhajans*. It is a different story altogether that after a sitting or two, Tina got bored of the whole thing, started yawning, and limited her role to that of blowing the conch-shell when it was time for *aarti*.

The children were growing up, feelings of animosity also grew. Sonu, Tina's elder brother, went to fetch milk from the dairy everyday, and at times he hated getting up in the mornings, especially during winters.

'It is only I who fetch milk in the morning, Shraman is never asked to go.' Now this Shraman was Punnu's younger son.

Once Tina wrote in her diary, 'We are one brother and one sister.'

'Who told you that?' Sanjana, Punnu's daughter, asked her, 'I thought you were seven brothers and sisters.'

That included all the cousins, and Tina didn't know what to say. She was feeling quite ashamed, she didn't know how to defend herself, so she said, 'My mother told me.

Bama, Punnu's son, sat on that stool in the verandah, placed at the extreme corner, and revised his lessons. He was feeling sleepy, he had studied quite late at night, and he went inside for that short nap. A thief tried sneaking into the house, and he had almost succeeded in taking away the stool with him, if it was not for Bama. Bama, as luck would have it, came back, his eyes heavy with sleep, he wanted to take his book inside. He spotted the thief and raised an alarm. The thief ran away, he thought of trying his luck again some other time.

They were from a middle class family, didn't have a lot of money, children had to be fed, educated, they tried to save on several heads so that the household could run smoothly. The monthly ration of wheat was bought from the government-controlled ration shop which sold it at a subsidised rate. All the children were required to clean it of stones. One who could collect the maximum number of stones got appreciation. In fact, it was with some pride that Vishakha, the eldest female cousin, showed the small mound of stones, white, black and grey, multi-coloured, that she had collected. Seeing that, her mother, Godavari, her face glowing with pride, said,

'Look at the kind of training I have given to my daughters! If only some people learnt by it!' Though this speech was addressed to none in particular, Sharda knew it was meant for her.

Godavari was a great one at making pickles. In the evenings, when he returned from his office, Punnu would, at times, come back, his bicycle handle loaded with the green, raw mangoes. Punnu would enter the gate of the house, one of the children would run to remove the bag containing the raw mangoes, Punnu would lift his bicycle with both hands, carefully avoiding the *chowki* which was kept right there, in the verandah, where Punnu sat in the evenings and rubbed his body till the dirt came out, black as soot, which Punnu then collected in his palm and threw it in the semicircular dust bin that they had placed at the extreme corner of the courtyard. The next day, after the children were all off to school, Punnu and Tunnu had gone to their respective places of work- one to his office and the other to his workshop- and Sharda had taken up her book, Godavari would squat on the ground, and start peeling the raw mangoes. She could work and speak at the same time.

'These things one can't have with money,' she observed, loud enough so that her voice reached Sharda who was busy preparing for her medical entrance test. Sharda was a very good student, Punnu's wife knew that, and she knew that Sharda would not have much difficulty in clearing the entrance test. Sharda, the doctor, she knew, would earn a lot, once she set up her own practice, and it was this Sharda, the doctor, whom she wanted to tell a thing or two. While preparing the *masala*, her hands yellow with the turmeric she had touched, Godavari continued her monologue.

'My mother trained me so well, mind you, I come from a family of *zamindars*, in my father's house I didn't take a glass of water myself, we had servants for that, but still see the kind of training my mother gave me! I can cook, I can knit, I can make pickles!' She was, by now, filling the mouth of mango, cut on all four sides, with its bottom intact, and this needed a bit of concentration, so she decided to give a break to her monologue.

Sharda was, by now, sufficiently provoked. She shut the book in her hand, put it on the table with a loud bang, and charging out of the room, with the towel in hand, she entered the bathroom, throwing an angry look at Punnu's wife, who knew that she should stop, and decided to resume her monologue later on.

Tunnu's wife passed the medical entrance test. Her husband was happy, even Punnu was happy. He felt proud of his sister-in-law. Sharda applied for a seat in the hostel. Her children, Tina and Sonu, visited her on Sundays. The first thing that they did when they reached their mother's room was to look at the jars, those plastic ones their mother had bought, in which she kept all kinds of eatables her children were interested in. After that, they were required to open their books. And this was what Sonu was not much interested in. His sister was the *rattoo* kind, one who mugged up almost the entire syllabus, and with her Sharda did not have much of a problem. But Sonu was different. When Sharda gave him dictation, his hands started aching only after writing one paragraph. Sharda would press his hands for a few minutes before Sonu was in a mood to resume. At times Sonu would climb onto the tin shed.

'Promise that you won't teach me. Only then will I get down.' Sharda, concerned for her son's safety, who stood dangerously on the tin shed, had to say,

'Come down, I promise not to teach you any more today.'

'Not even tomorrow?' Sonu was growing bolder. He never knew his bargaining powers with his mother were so good.

'O. k., o.k.' Sharda gave up.

Bama and Sharda, Bama's aunt, were almost contemporaries. He was also a medical student. *Mai* was boasting before *Panditayan,* her rival and neighbour, one whose husband had been a great friend of *Babu, Mai's* husband, at one point of time, but a dispute over where *Panditayan,* now a neighbour, got the bathroom constructed, much against the wishes of *Mai* and *Babu,* had done much damage to that friendship. So as I said, *Mai* was boasting before *Panditayan,*

'Now I have three doctors in the family.'

'Name them,' *Panditayan* challenged, confident that *Mai* had made some mistake somewhere.

'O.k.,' *Mai* began, counting on her fingers, 'my younger daughter-in-law, Sharda, Punnu's eldest son, Bama, and my younger daughter, Suchitra.'

Panditayan was now smiling. She knew Suchitra's mother had been wrong all along.

'And when did Suchitra become a doctor?' *Panditayan,* whose sons had done well for themselves, her one granddaughter was in the Indian Police Service, another was studying in the Cambridge University, knew that now it was she who had had the upper hand. 'Suchitra is a nurse, not a doctor,' she was smiling, 'when will you understand that?'

Mai felt humiliated. She asked Tina, her youngest granddaughter, her hand on her chin, 'Is it correct? Is not your aunt a doctor?' Tina didn't feel like hurting her grandmother, so she said she didn't know.

Mai claimed to have read the whole of *Ramayan* from one end to the other though when Tina asked her grandmother to write her name, she said she wouldn't, her eyesight had deteriorated.

Panditayan laughed. *Mishraji's* children are all educated but none of them have done well in life. *Mai* certainly did not like *Panditayan* for this. When this *Pandit* and *Panditayan* had no where to go to, I had given them shelter. Now look at the manner in which she boasts in front of me, *Mai* would sit and mutter.

The days they sold old newspapers, they had fish in the evenings. Fish market was near, their house was on the banks of river *Ganga.* They got fish from the market, the scales they had at home were taken out, the fish was weighed again, and if it was discovered that the fisher woman gave hundred grams less of fish, they would be angry. They would go back to the market and come back with those extra one hundred grams. Then those special *masalas* would be ground on the grinding stone they kept in front of the kitchen. When the smell of *masala* being fried reached the children, they would all be in a hurry to finish with their homework. They knew that as soon as they finished their homework, they would get their dinner. The pan with fish would be still on the earthen oven so that it didn't get cold.

Mai had a great temper. The matriarch of the house, with *Babu* dead, she wielded power. It was *Babu's* death anniversary, she had invited some of her co-villagers, now settled in Patna, and the family members- male family members- of both her daughters-in-law. Tunnu's wife had two brothers, one was young and the other grown up. When once Tunnu's wife asked her younger brother, the latter, to wish the librarian, he said, his hands on his hips,

'I don't say good morning to every Tom, Dick and Harry.'

So somehow this brother of Tunnu's wife forgot to come on this occasion. *Mai* did not like it. Sharda's mother, a beautiful and benign lady, one who never disobeyed her husband when she lived, sent a jackfruit, big and ripe, which Sharda's elder brother, Tina's Peelu *Mama,* brought in a *rickshaw,* and while he was searching his pocket for some coins, *Mai,* who normally sat in the verandah, got up, her eyes shining with anger, and said,

'Peelu, just take this jackfruit back this instant.'

Peelu did not know what hit him.

Anyway, he had to take the jackfruit back. And he remembered *Mai* for a long time for this.

Leena, Godavari's daughter, also had an uncle in Patna- *Lal Mama.* He was not red in colour, actually in those parts where they came from, *Lal* was considered nice. Actually, his name was Bhola, Bhola *Mama.* He had quite a few children. Once in two-three months, Bhola *Mama's* family would come, all loaded in two *rickshaws* – they would stay in the house for the afternoon, the children would play, the aunts would gossip. When it was time for them to go back, in the evening, when sky darkened, and they thought it wouldn't be advisable to be late, hot *paranthas* with *bhujia*- potatoes cut into small, thin strips, which would then be fried in oil- would be prepared. They would all then feast on those *paranthas* and *bhujia* and set off, promising to repeat the visit. Of course, Leena and company had to pay back the visit first.

Whenever Tina and Sonu would go their *Nani's* place, their maternal grandmother's, they would stay there for a day or two. Tina's school was just across the road, and in the evenings they would go to her school, ride on the merry-go-round, and have a lot of fun. At times Tina would spot Mrs. Singh, their English teacher, one who wore different colours of lipstick everyday. She would sit there, near the swings, where her youngest daughter would be playing, and correct the copybooks she had carried from the classroom.

When they came back, the first thing that *Mai* would ask was, 'what did your *Nani* give you to eat?'

Tina and Sonu had strict instructions from their mother to say that they had *halwa-poori* although they often had potato sandwich. *Halwa-poori* was considered rich at *Mai's* place, it had a place which potato sandwich could never take.

Tunnu, *Mai's* son, was a good player, his room was full of trophies he had won when playing football, in athletics, in 100m race. Being the athletic type, tall and of a strong built, no one tangled with Tunnu in his locality. When there would be a fight, Tunnu, the athlete, would jump, flexing his muscles, shouting all the while. Anyway, he never really had to show his physical prowess for when he shouted, it was enough, and no one had the inclination to test his physical strength.

The children of Punnu and Tunnu were growing up, Sharda did not like all this. 'What example are you setting in front of your children? What will they learn? They will never respect you for this.' But the brothers were not bothered.

Sharda had almost finished with her medical course, she took the final examination, passed it, and then, immediately thereafter, started making preparation for the M.S. entrance test. She was concerned for her children. In a year or two they would take the Board examinations. After her M.S., Sharda got a posting in an adjoining town and she commuted to and fro on a train for one or two years. Tina and Sonu took their Board examinations, she called them to the place where she was posted, asked them to lock themselves in a room and study hard. Both the children did well, got admission in Delhi where they pursued their further studies. They came back only during the vacations, most of the time just before their examinations. Sharda saw to it they studied hard. Their father was more liberal, he would call the children and ask them to watch TV when his wife was asleep.

'Just now she has gone off to sleep,' he would say, grinning, his big teeth- something his daughter had got from him-shining. The children would put away their books and follow him to the drawing room where they would watch TV.

Mai died. She was cremated at *Baans Ghat.* Sharda, well established in her practice, left the house with her own family. Godavari got all her sons and daughters married, they set up their own families. Most of the children left the house.

The Fat Woman

Kamli was not beautiful. And she knew it. Neither did she have any pretensions about her looks- tall, dark and commonplace. Jogna, her husband, would sometimes tease her saying that small children would not throw tantrums if they were shown Kamli's face at night; her flared nostrils, protruding teeth and a tall, inky frame, was demon-like. Not that Kamli minded it. Or even if she did, there was no way we could find it out for Kamli had other worries.

I have known Kamli since I was a child. She came to look after *Pujama*, my grandmother. Being frail and thin, her bones brittle like twigs, *Pujama* was unable to look after herself in the evening of her life. So she wrote to her brother in Navanagar that she would require the services of an old and trusted matron. Whatever she said was law to her brother who immediately started making preparations for Kamli's departure. 'Huh', his daughter-in-law commented, 'She never looked at us a second time after she left for Patna. But how *Babuji* prostrates himself before her. And that also before a step-sister', was her parting shot.

Never ever will I know as vociferous a supporter of bonded labour as Kamli was. It was irritating for me to hear her constantly harp about the protection provided by the *Haakim*- the *zamindar*- to her family. 'What humbug', I would retort for I had heard the *zamindars* were ruthless and cruel. Papa had told me all this. And Papa can never be wrong. 'No *Bucchi,*' Kamli would say, her eyes moist with tears, her mouth moving like that of a buffalo's, 'those days! After Jogna died, I had lost all faith in God. When Sukhni came and informed me about my poor Jogna's death, I started beating at my belly. So violently that I lost the child I had carried and it was a son! A son! It was your great grandfather, may his soul rest in peace, who ensured that the two girls and I do not die of hunger. "Kamli, take a sack of rice and ask your mistress to give you some pulses; do not starve your family to death." He was so benevolent....', at this Kamli would burst into a torrent of tears. I would slip away, leaving Kamli to her past.

Kamli was a big sycophant. She hated moving her fat body around and aware of her limitation, she had mastered the art of buttering. Many a time I would see her lying prostrate on the ground but the moment Ma or Papa were in sight, Kamli would swing into action. 'Hey you', she would chide her fellow servant, 'when will you learn to sweep properly? I can see so much of dust in that corner. You must improve or I would have to report about your inefficiency'. Saying so she would start cleaning and engage herself in the task of removing the invisible dust. 'She has become the manager of the house', my grandmother would mutter. When she would order Kamli to get up and assist her in going to the bathroom- for my grandmother's digestive system had become weak with age- she would in turn pass on the order to the maid sleeping next to her. 'Get up, she is calling you', saying so she would doze off.

And how sweet tongued she was. Kamli knew how her interests were best served. '*Bucchi*, you wear such beautiful frocks,' she would tell me, in her thick syrupy voice, examining the frock I wore, 'my poor granddaughter can not afford such nice frocks and she is your age.' Then she would pretend to look at my frock minutely, 'but I can see a small hole here.' A moment's silence. 'A kid like you should not wear such torn frocks. I must talk to your mother about it.' Kamli would not rest till she had secured my frock for her granddaugher. Often I would hear her telling Ma how poor she was and how all her *sarees* were torn. Any new *saree* thus obtained, after sufficiently rousing Ma's compassion, would be shoved in the big bag she had. My brother and I would peep into Kamli's bag just before she was about to leave for her village. We would find the old sieve Ma had asked her to throw, the pair of trousers Papa had worn on *Holi* and were of no use to him now, the *sarees* our Ma had given to her on festivals, our discarded toys, all found place in Kamli's bag. 'Bina,' my brother would joke, 'shall I throw Kamli's bag in the drain one day and see what she does on seeing her things thus thrown?' Somehow he never had the heart to do so.

'*Didi*', once Kamli asked my grandmother, her eyes glued to my grandmother's fingers, 'if I serve you selflessly, will you give that golden ring that you wear in your small finger to me when you die?'

'When will this greedy woman leave me? Oh God, and she says she will serve me selflessly.'

Kamli loved eating. Especially when fish was cooked. Everyone knew that Kamli always hid a portion of whatever was cooked at home for her consumption. Many a time she had been pulled up for being greedy. But incorrigible that she was, she would invent new methods of hiding things and eating stealthily. 'Eat, Kamli, but not like this,' everyone would tell her. Not like what? she would wonder. The moment the pan was placed on the gas stove and the smell of anything being cooked assailed her nostrils, Kamli would go mad. She was often tempted to eat from the pan itself. 'We are such lucky Brahmins', my brother would joke, 'we eat the leftovers of our cook.' The day on which all this was reported to Papa and after Papa had sufficiently taken her to task, the complainant had had it. 'You jealous creature, you barren woman, you, who has a black tongue, may you never be in peace! This is the curse of a widow, a pious widow about whose virtue and truthfulness they still talk about in her village. For the whole village of Navanagar knows how virtuous I am. How can they forget the day the whole of Navanagar was flooded and it was I, Kamli, who swam to *Haakim's* place- *Haakim*, who was always so good to me (here Kamli shed a few tears in memory of her *Haakim*)- and saved all the sacks of wheat and rice from perishing. I, who have been so faithful to my masters, have to see this day!' at this she banged her forehead. My brother looked at me and smiled. 'And everyone has forgotten the day those thieves had entered this house, such deadly ones at that, and when this woman who is grinning at me so shamelessly, had hidden behind me for safety. Coward that she is, she has the cheek to give such reports against me!' and Kamli went on and on.

We loved peeping into Kamli's plate to discover fresh proofs of her gluttony. Had it been possible, she would have eaten and digested the share of each one of us and would have found nothing wrong with it. 'Let it be', Ma would say, 'she did not get enough to eat back at her home, let her have her fill here. At least she is loyal to us; where do we get such servants nowadays?'

Whenever Kamli would go to her village she would return after spending a month or two with her daughters. She was an unlucky woman. While Ghurni, her elder daughter, had six children and a husband who was always drunk, her second daughter, Sushila, was insane. But Kamli was clever. She somehow managed to get Sushila married to a boy from a faraway village where the report of her insanity had not reached. As was expected, the girl was deserted by her husband the moment he found the truth but then Kamli's purpose had been well served. Her daughter was carrying. Kamli heaved a sigh of relief. 'At least her child will be there to look after her when I am dead', she would sigh. It was poverty that made Kamli collect bits and scraps so that she could go to her village and hand them over to her daughters.

Once Kamli had sent a money order of three thousand rupees and instructed her elder daughter to pay off a portion of debt due to the moneylender; Kamli had spent lavishly on her second daughter's wedding. Sushila, her second daughter, wanted to keep that money to herself. 'My husband has sent this money to me, you liar, so that I can buy *sarees*; you are a jealous creature and that is why you refuse to hand over my money to me.' Ghurni was highly irritated. 'Huh, has your husband ever come to see you? And you say he has sent money for you!' When all this was narrated to Kamli, she smiled sadly. 'What will she do, poor soul? Ghurni, you must not make your sister feel small.'

Oh, it seems I have lost track of what I was saying. Yes. Kamli would return from her village. Thin and emaciated. It was as if a child had pricked a pin into the thick, sooty bag filled with water.

'Kamli has become a bag of bones,

Kamli who was so fat and had a big nose'.

I would clap and break into a song the moment I would see Kamli thus transformed. 'Kamli, Kamli, where has your tummy gone?'

'She has handed that over to her daughters,' my brother would join in. Kamli would smile and say nothing. She did not mind what we children said. But this was not so with the others. When the other maid insulted her by pointing towards her torn *saree*, she immediately put her in place. 'That is because I have daughters to look after, stupid woman! How can I remain in finery while they are in tatters! But how would you know, barren woman!'

The barren woman was furious. She went and gave Ma a detailed account of Kamli's fresh attempts to fatten herself. And fattened she was. With renewed vigour Kamli would devote herself to boss around and establish her importance. *Pujama* would hate all this.

'Have you come here to take care of me or to boss around?'

'But *didi* this is part of my job', she would say, 'if I do not keep an eye on this barren woman, she would waste everything. But I would not allow her to do such a thing. Poor Memsahib, she is so busy. She hardly has time to eat (here she would sigh) but I am here to manage her household. Faithful that I am, I would not let this one waste anything.'

Kamli would also report to Ma about the other maid's amorous activities. At nights when Ma would come home, very tired after a hard day's work, and would flop on her bed, Kamli would present herself with a bowl full of mustard oil. In all earnestness, she would start massaging Ma. And how my mother loved it. It is then that Kamli would open her bag of stories. 'Memsahib', she looked around to make sure no one was around, 'this woman in the house, the serpent, how do I tell you what she is up to nowadays!' At this she would cover her ears as if the very sound of the woman's name would pollute Kamli who was so pious, so religious. 'It was one o' clock in the morning or was it two or three (at this Kamli would look confused) when I woke up suddenly on hearing some body's footsteps. I saw the fallen woman unlatching the door softly and leaving the room in a hurry, Memsahib! I followed her, softly, step by step. *Hare Rama! Hare Rama*! How do I tell you where she went! She was with that new servant Sharma Memsahib, our neighbour, has engaged, and who sleeps on the verandah. But I can not give you further details,' and she threw a meaningful glance at Ma only to find that Ma had already gone off to sleep. Not certain whether Ma had heard the core portion of her story, she picked up her bowl of oil and swore she would repeat the story the next day for Ma's benefit.

Then one day Kamli saw on television that the whole of Darbhanga had been inundated. *'Ghurni ho-o-o, Sushila ho-o-o,'* she started beating her breast, 'whom did I have to call my own after your *Babu* left for his heavenly abode save for you two! Floods in the village and you can not even swim. With *Haakim* dead, who will look after you two in my absence! Ghurni....' Then Kamli fell headlong on the floor, crying, kicking her legs, occasionally throwing a glance at Papa to see what effect all this had on him. For the next few days, she was inconsolable.

Papa thought it best to send her home the moment the floods had subsided. It was a much better option than to listen to Kamli raving and ranting. But Kamli did not forget to stuff her bag with things this time too. She was very practical. Ever since Jogna had died, her instinct of survival had become acute. This time we, children, did not play any pranks on her, well aware of her plight. But thankfully nothing happened to her family and Kamli was back with us within a week.

To her consternation, Kamli found that the other maid had grown in importance in her absence; this Kamli could not stand. 'This lazy bug, this good for nothing woman, I tell you Memsahib, one day this woman is going to sell you off and she will have no qualms about it. This woman prepares much more food than is required and where do the leftovers go? In the gutter, where else? She wastes so much. With none to take care of my poor Memsahib's household, this woman had her way. But don't you worry, now that Kamli is here, she will take care.'

'Yes, of course, the great manager has come to manage the household,' *Pujama* muttered, eyeing Kamli's buttocks, a small hillock.

'*Didi*, you don't have faith in me. You, for whose family we have spent our lives! Don't you remember when you wanted to go around on the elephant, *Haakim* could think of none but my father-in-law to take care of you! "Rodhia, I can not think of anyone but you who can look after my daughter; she wants to move around in the village on our elephant. Be with her." But *didi*, I know you have started disliking me nowadays. You have forgotten our good deeds. Oh, how could I forget, it is time to give fruit juice to Memsahib. I must rush.'

'My child, the masters of those days were so nice,' Kamli would tell me stories. 'They thought it was their duty to feed us. If anyone of us had become an invalid and was no longer fit to work, they wouldn't discard us like the present day employers. We would become their dependants, just like an invalid child. But those were days! By the way, do you have some change?'

'Why?'

She grinned. 'I have exhausted my stock of *bidis*; I feel like having one badly. But don't tell your Ma about it.'

'Smoking is bad. Why don't you quit this dirty habit?'

'Ah,' Kamli would start again, her forehead furrowed, 'When Jogna died, I felt like killing myself. Once when I sat in front of my house, cursing myself and telling Sugni, my neighbour, how I hated living, Sugni gave me a suggestion. She said that when things become unbearable, I should smoke a *bidi* to relieve the tension, for nothing could give more comfort, she said. And thus, I started smoking. It does help, after all,' she confided. Kamli took the money and bought a few bundles of *bidis* for herself. At night, I could hear her coughing very badly. Ma was furious. 'This woman consumes medicines like chocolates but can not leave her *bidi*. Who gave you money to buy them?' Ma asked Kamli. 'No body,' she said, 'I found a crumpled five-rupee note lying in the bathroom and I picked that up.'

'Now she has started stealing too,' Ma was muttering, 'had she not been an old servant I would have kicked her out this instant.'

'Oh child, I thought I have had it,' Kamli was telling me soon afterwards, her teeth shining, 'for your Ma really has a temper; but I was able to get out of it, wasn't I?' she was smiling.

'But Kamli you lied,' I told her.

'Lied!' she said, 'these are big words my child! When you have to struggle to survive in this world, these words don't have any meaning for you.'

Last time when I went home, I heard Kamli was dead.

Two Chairs

Up and down, up and down. I wanted to tire myself so that I did not have the time to think of anything. That was my strategy, to tire myself to such an extent that I did not need to think of anything but my tiredness. Or, maybe I would have gone to the bathroom and poured mugs and mugs of water on myself and, believe me, it does have a cooling effect. Or, there was another option. I would leave the house and start walking aimlessly till my feet hurt, they would swell, and would hardly fit into my tiny shoes, and then I would decide it was time to go home. Home where there was a fan, a bed, and two rickety chairs, always ready to give in under the weight of a slightly heavy man. I did not have the money to buy better chairs; and I was quite satisfied with them. Till I saw those chairs.

Money has power. You can buy love, you can buy education, you can buy power, and of course, two nice, proper chairs. Nice and red. The kind I saw in the shop the other day. The kind I desperately wanted for myself.

Let me recollect what led to the fight. I remember getting up in the evening after the siesta and sitting on those good, old rickety chairs. They creaked under the weight of my body though I did not mind. The newspaper was full of reports that could catch my attention—match-fixing, brawl in a leading club, the Indian influence in the IT world, commentary of a leading environmentalist etc., etc. When I turned to the fourth page, there was something printed at the right hand corner, towards the end, which caught my attention. It was an advertisement which showed two chairs, red in colour, the chairs I have already discussed above, the chairs that would then onward give me sleepless nights. I talked to my husband about them, he said he had no money. We really did not have the money. I tried hard to sleep that night but could not. The chairs kept haunting me all night.

At the break of dawn I got up, wrapped a shawl around myself, took my purse and stuffed some currency notes in it, crumpled ten rupee notes, and went to my friend's place. There was a big padlock hanging on the door, staring at me, mockingly. But I was not going to give in so easily. I went straight to my sister's place from there and requested her to help me in buying those chairs. 'Why? The chairs that you have are good enough for the two of you!' she exclaimed, and shut the door on my face. I was not surprised, she has always been like this—rough, brusque and hard-hearted. She did not even invite me in for a cup of tea, normal courtesy one would extend even to a mere acquaintance.

I remained undeterred. This time I went to my aunt's place, she was sitting in her well manicured garden, a riot of colours, and playing with her furry friend, Snoopy. Snoopy came running to me; I gave her a friendly pat. I wonder why all the dogs here have English names, Snoopy, Snoovy, Lucy, and why not say, Sharada, Sarasvati, Mrinalini. I could see my aunt had new, diamond bracelets that looked like small, white blobs on the circular ring. 'Your uncle got them from the US for me,' she said. Well, I seized the opportunity to talk to her about the chairs. I told her how beautiful the chairs were and that ever since I had set my eyes upon them, I had lost my sleep. What ensued was a long lecture on the laws of economics and the necessity to live within ones means. Having summed up the fundamentals of survival thus, she rose to call up her daughter now settled in the US. 'Don't worry, darling,' I overheard her telling her daughter, 'buy the house in the best locality. After all, why does your father earn so much?' I knew it was time for me to leave. But where to go? To the house with a bed, a fan, and two rickety chairs, the chairs that I desperately wanted to replace.

I remembered my parents. They were loveable who did not live long to love me.

As orphans, my sister and I lived with our aunt and, of course, Snoopy. So while Snoopy and my cousin, who is now in the U. S., got the best in life, my sister and I got to know what it was like to be an orphan. Just like those two rickety chairs, the chairs that creaked under the weight of a slightly heavy man sitting. My cousin and Snoopy shone like the two bright chairs I desperately wanted to possess.

As a child I had ample opportunity to know the difference between the nice, glossy chairs and old, rickety chairs- while the frocks remained new and glossy, they were my cousin's and after that they were all mine. Once I cried and asked for a new frock, sky blue in colour with pink birds embroidered on it, and a white, satin belt. My aunt was amazed. So habituated was she to our compliance that it took her quite some time to digest what had happened. She decided she had to be strict otherwise the children would be spoilt. I had to remain without food and water for two days. My sister had smirked. 'You got it,' she seemed to say. And I was convinced. I really did deserve it.

When a child, I had gone to the local municipality school, across the road, which was five minutes' walk from where I lived, wearing *salwar kurta* with a *dupatta* which was white in colour. My aunt had to pay ten rupees as my school fee every month, quite a paltry sum against the fee paid for my cousin's education. She went to the most expensive school in the town, dressed in a blue, pleated skirt, white blouse, black shoes and grey socks. I would look at her wistfully. I did cry occasionally when I saw my aunt play with my cousin in the evenings, and remembered my own mother whom I had hidden in my trunk, in a photo frame. Since most of the time I was busy doing household chores, I did not get much time to wallow in self-pity.

And then I grew up. Suddenly. In fact, not so suddenly, for I could remember hundreds of such instances before I grew up, my cousin going to the USA for a degree in Business Administration, my sister eloping with someone at the age of thirteen, Snoopy getting old and my aunt older. But I never dared to question my aunt after the frock episode, not even when talking about the chairs, good old chairs, so dear to my heart.

My husband was very fond of me, so much so that he was ready to give up his life for me. Once I had spilled tea on my body, with steam rising like silver ribbons from the surface. I was casually holding the handle of the teacup, engrossed in some conversation, and somehow the teacup tilted slightly, and its entire content fell on my bosom. I started shrieking, unable to bear the pain. When I cried, he too cried. There was this special bonding between us. I knew there was somebody who loved me. My mother had also loved me; but, of course, she did not live long. At times I took out her photograph, and looked at her intently; did God really need her more than I did? I doubted. But that is what my husband told me.

Unfortunately we were poor, not that I was very demanding but somehow this time I could not get over those chairs. He was the only ray of hope now. I broached the topic again, after tea in the evening, when the sun was an orange ball, the colour of my daughter's lollypop, and we had taken a walk for about half an hour; he expressed his helplessness again, his savings could not cover half the cost of the chairs, those lovely darlings. This time I was cruel, very cruel, and hurt him where it hurt the most. I pointed out how worthless he was, good for nothing. I shouted at him and he at me. I abused him and he flung the hairbrush he held in his hands at me, cutting my chin. I caught hold of his right arm and twisted it, he squeaked in pain, I relented and released him. Thereafter I left the house.

By now I was very angry. I felt like throttling myself in desperation. But I was never like this before. I wonder what has happened to me, I am becoming more and more militant day by day. It is difficult for me to control my anger, I lose my cool at the slightest provocation. That is why I have devised methods to control my anger- like running up and down the stairs, walking aimlessly for several hours on desolate streets, in the dead of night.

The chairs. When I slept I saw them, when I woke up, I saw them. I can not explain why.

I returned home at one o'clock in the morning, very tired. My husband was sitting in the balcony, staring at the star-less sky, a blank sheet of paper. Pushing him a bit, I sat beside him. He handed over the money to me, several hundred rupees, and asked me to count them. I looked at him. I was amazed. Where did he get so much of money from? I thought about those chairs and I was thrilled. I saw, in my dream, I went to the Shopping Mall, gave the money to the shopkeeper, and took what I had dreamt of day and night for the past few days.

Exactly at ten o'clock, I was at the shop. I could see the shop boy sweeping and scrubbing the floor and arranging the articles to be sold in the course of the day. I looked at him and then tried to hand over the money across the counter. 'I am sorry,' the fat man sitting across the counter was apologetic, 'they were sold yesterday.'

The Change

She had turned religious. All of a sudden? No, gradually. In fact the change had come stealthily and had been so subtle that she was amazed. When in college she loved to be associated with the students' wing of Marxist Party, the party of the poor, seeking to do away with the inequality inherent in the system. She would get up in the mornings, splash her face with water, slip on the *khadi kurta* and the blue pair of jeans she had been wearing everyday that week, and on which brown patches of dirt could easily be detected, and march onwards.

Left-right-left. Left-right-left. Salute Comrade Ashwini. March onward. So much has to be done. The entire burden of bringing about the radical change was on her. The street plays. *Suno-suno-suno. Dham-dham-dham-dham-dham.* Ten to fifteen students gathered along with one or two street urchins. No elaborate costumes. No makeup. A shawl was draped over the jeans she wore. A bag was slung over the shoulder for the effect. Some shouted, some raved and some ranted. At the end they all sang in chorus. With a vision in their eyes. All had future in their eyes.

Religion is the opium of the masses. What humbug!

She has got a small *mandir* constructed in her house with *Ganesh* on one side and *Laxmi* on the other. She likes the comforts of life, her ambition knowing no limit. And she gets angry when anyone talks ill of her religion. Every morning she makes it a point to spend at least thirty minutes before the idols of various gods and goddesses and recite the *mantras* she knows. She has realized the importance of things material and the vital role the idols seem to play in their acquisition.

No. Don't think she has forgotten the poor and the downtrodden. In fact on the red lights, while going to her workplace, when she is accosted by small children begging and asking for a one rupee coin, you know she has full sympathies for them, especially for the really small and vulnerable ones, she immediately fishes for some stray coins. In fact once or twice she paused. No, no. Father Marx would not like all this. He was strictly against such bourgeois gestures, delaying the inevitable. Anyway she would shrug and drive away. Now she has stopped being a visionary. She is now firm in her conviction that she can not change the world, but she can at least give small pleasures.

The bright smile on the face of the child with the running nose makes her day.

Black Robes

Young. A very young man. With a flat, plateau-like nose and eyebrows that were jointed. He acquired a degree in law from Campus Law Centre, Delhi University, where he drank tea flavoured with cardamom, served in small glass tumblers, and brought by *Chotu*, a child aged six to seven years, who could be seen running around with his iron container. It had a number of slots in which five to six glasses could be placed at one time.

Chotu was swift and agile. He always ran like one who had to catch the 2:30 bus but had left the house at 2:28. Any order placed by the students was immediately attended by him. So while the young man, then barely twenty-one or twenty-two, finished with his classes and headed towards the Bunnilal tea stall, with his assortment of friends, *Chotu* ran with three glasses, filled with tea, towards him.

Once he forgot to pay Bunnilal. He had to hurry up, his father had come, he was alone in his small bachelor's room, with a cot and a fan, and he had to accompany him to the Emporium from where he could buy *sarees* for his mother. And he forgot to pay Bunnilal. Very interesting. His father had smiled. You are developing all the traits of a lawyer. The black man in the black robes. He knew his father's penchant for cracking jokes.

Carefree. Careless. He mounted the steps of the Supreme Court and felt his heart swell with pride. Dressed in black jeans and a white T-shirt, with John Lennon staring at the tricolour, fluttering over the chief's head, he reached the tall, black gates. He wore a black coat, the band and then the gown. But, it seemed, there was some fundamental flaw somewhere. The others stared at him, and soon he realized what the problem was. You can wear a long black skirt but not a short one. No T-shirt with John Lennon. It had to be a white shirt with cuff links. Formal lawyers in formal dresses addressing the court in a formal manner.

Exasperating. He would mutter. Enter the courtroom and bow down and address the chair in the old, feudal style. Why 'My Lords', why not 'Sir', or better still, why not Mr. Chatterjee or Mr. Sikri or Mr. Parekh. But it would be most interesting, he thought, the very thought bringing a smile to his thick, cigarette stained lips, to call them by their first names. What is wrong with it? C'mon Jeevan, he imagined himself, standing, his papers on the table, the judges looking at him intently, why don't you see sense? No contempt, please. He certainly disapproved of those who threw *chappals* at the Bench, but c'mon, it is high time things changed.

The young man, idealistic, unaware of the world and its treacheries, started working under a senior lawyer. *Guru-shishya parampara.* The pupil with a John Lennon T-shirt and the *Guru,* pompous but good at heart. The *Guru* would teach him the tricks of the trade. What tricks? I had joined a profession! The *Guru* would give up. Learn law, child, he would explain, this time he would be gentle, explaining slowly and patiently, but there are other things too. For example? Ok, I will explain. The *Guru's* voice was now at the lowest pitch, he had assumed the poise of a *swami*, though what he said was more familiar to a marketing man on the corporate side, the man with a coat and tie, with a capacity to sell dirt in the name of gold. The client is like a child, he explained, and you have to draw his attention towards yourself. There may be hundreds of lawyers like you, in fact more capable and more sharp, but the client, that is the child, has to be attracted, enticed.

There was a toy-seller. He worked very hard and made beautiful toys. He made them and then dressed them in colourful dresses and made tiny shoes of all colours, rounded and sharp edged. Then he would put them in a basket covering them with a dirty piece of cloth and would sit in the village market and shout, 't-o-y-s, t-o-y-s.' None would come, the poor man could hardly survive; his earnings were meagre. His daughter- a thin, undernourished child with eyes that were corpse-like - would clutch one of the toys every day and go off to sleep, always getting lesser and lesser to eat with each passing day. Then one day the toy-seller lost the piece of cloth with which he covered his toys and his daughter playfully stuck red and green and yellow wrappers someone had thrown on the road, on the toys, and hurray! Children flocked to his basket that day. Such lovely toys, they would marvel, and compel their parents to buy more than one toy.

'One for me and one for Chintu,' they would try to convince, pulling their parents towards the toy-seller, and walk away with the toys. That day the toy-seller was very happy. He had sold all his toys.

Likewise, explained the *Guru*, I may know law, but unless I am able to show myself as a competent lawyer, my talents are of no use. So in the beginning, like the toy-seller, the lawyer has to learn the tricks of attracting the clients and there are several ways of doing that. What followed was not particularly pleasant and the young man muttered *Hari Om! Hari Om!* and left the place.

The young man went home a disturbed man. He had read his books in college thoroughly. While others roamed around, sat in the college canteen, or loitered around, he sat in the college library and increased the power of his lenses by straining his eyes over some case law or some statutory provision. He was fairly rewarded in college, he passed with distinction in every subject and he dreamt of becoming one of the topmost lawyers one day, one who appeared in several cases everyday and charged a hefty sum, the sum that only the bigwigs in industry and the real rich could afford. At that time he was not aware that for this he needed talents other than what he already had. Marketing strategies, something they taught only in the IIMs and in other such institutions. Something the lawyers were supposed to, under the rules, shun. A lawyer advertising himself! Unethical. Barred.

In the courtrooms he listened with rapt attention the arguments and counter arguments. He saw the 'green' lawyer in the court room. The passion of the green lawyer with anything green was so pronounced that he would even support South Africa in a cricket match against India only for the reason that the South Africans wore green jerseys. He was the darling of the activists of the green movement, who preferred to see everything with their green tinted glasses even though the things had started turning red. But there was nothing green about his robes or his papers. They were the right colour. It was only his reputation that was green. The television-*wallahs* and the newspaper-*wallahs* were ready to click him and cover him. They knew the power of the colour green and did not want to miss out on anything that was newsworthy.

Once the young man got the opportunity to argue, he being fresh and therefore not being competent to handle the matter notwithstanding; the case was intricate, involving complexities, worth being argued for hours at length and calling for re-examination of the entire case. He was delighted. With a pat on his back and a slight push on his bums, he found himself standing before the Bench, the toughest one, the one that resounded with thunderous, 'Are we sitting under a banyan tree and dispensing justice?'

He mumbled, 'I have to make four submissions,' his white hands shaking, his eyes fixed on the nose of the Presiding Judge. Slightly hawkish, he felt.

'Yes counsel, kindly make your four submissions,' the Presiding judge smiled, his white and black hair neatly plastered to his scalp.

He muttered My Lords a few times with a few words thrown here and there and then again concentrated on the tip of the nose of the Presiding Judge.

'Anything more?'

'No, no,' he mumbled, how could he say any thing more?

'Dismissed. Next.'

He had a friend. Jeet Singh. O Jeeta, he would call him endearingly. Jeeta and he were great friends. He had acquired a locker in the court premises in which he kept his coat and band and gown after which they would go to the canteen, lash out at the boiling water with the tea bag, and vigorously stir sugar. Sugar, sugar, lots of sugar. Jeeta from Punjab liked his tea to be sweetened adequately with sugar while our young man was the intellectual type, black tea without sugar. JNU and its *latkas* and *jhatkas*. Jeeta had mentioned a month back that his wife was in Punjab but he intended to bring her to Delhi so that they could live together.

Now Jeeta was going through a bad patch. Just as the bank mistrusts the lawyer, considering him to be unworthy of credit and denying credit cards to him, the landlords too held Jeeta in utter disdain. Jeeta would leave the court and proceed immediately, in his black trousers and white shirt, pressing the doorbells of his prospective landlords, would meet with ill-luck and repeat this exercise the next day. Jeeta continued searching for accommodation for one full month after which he gave up. He went straight to Sardar Gurbachan Singh, his father-in-law, pressing his doorbell with all the force he could gather, and sitting in his living room, cross legged, he asked for a flat in Delhi as dowry, all the while looking at the bright and beautiful cushion covers Manjeet had embroidered. Manjeet, his wife. Sardar Gurbachan Singh had shown the cushion covers Manjeet had embroidered, the bed covers Manjeet had stitched, the wall painting Manjeet had painted, and tea that Manjeet had prepared. Jeeta decided that if anyone was talented in the family, it was Manjeet, if anyone worked in the family, it was Manjeet. Jeeta's problem was solved. He had a roof on his head. But his heart raged with anger when he remembered his attempts at acquiring a house on rent.

Our young man was idealistic and he did not believe in doing what Jeeta did. He had faith in himself and his talents.

He did not want to take the obligations of anyone, least of all the one he would marry or her family. But it did not take long before our man, his hairline receding, his face marked with lines that had made their appearance before time, totally disillusioned, gave up.

'Listen,' time for the *Guru* to step in, 'in this profession, unless you have a Godfather, a mentor, who regularly supports you and feeds you with the regular flow of cases, you are doomed.'

'And therefore,' the advice came free of cost, 'it is such people as your father and father-in-law, whose support should be sought in the initial years for survival.' Thus saying, the *Guru* stood up, scratching his head and making mental calculations, waiting for the client who had said he would be coming in the evening, but had not turned up till then.

'Jeeta, how much did you buy your flat for?'

Jeeta smiled. He said he had bought it for fifteen lakh rupees. 'Now, in fact,' Jeeta had said proudly, 'if you see my flat, slightly smaller accommodation than what you would expect, yet decorated in the most beautiful manner, you will truly like it.'

'In fact,' Jeeta said softly, in a velvety voice, 'I have got the balcony covered, and improvised an additional room.'

'Of course, it is against the building bye laws,' he added.

Jeeta. O Jeeta. Our young man would moan. 'You are in the wrong profession,' Jeeta would tell him. 'Why don't you leave it and go for a job?'

When the young man was young, that is, much younger than his present age, when one is headstrong, is not required to pay for the rents, can read and sleep when one wants to, go for night shows and can do other such similar things, he had read a book. In fact, the book was written by someone he had never heard of, but which he found so engrossing, that it compelled him to skip classes so that he could pore over its pages and absorb its contents. The book was written by a criminal lawyer, a court practitioner, one who penned down his experiences, his attempts at saving the lives of his clients, whether guilty or not, the nuances and the techniques, the arguments and the counter-arguments. In fact, the young man was so impressed by what he read that he took the decision to choose law as his vocation. Medical profession, noble profession. Legal profession, ignoble profession. All this did not deter him from becoming a lawyer.

His parents, of course, were very unhappy with this decision of his. One day, when he was still a student, in his sixth semester, he was strolling with his father in his hometown, Bulandshahar. He saw a man in torn shoes, looking like a crow fluttering on the road, a faded, black coat covering his chest. The trousers had black and white stripes.

'A lawyer,' his father had said.

They walked for sometime, hardly speaking, the honking buses speeding past them, some halting to load more passengers, despite the fact that those already on board hardly had any space to get a foothold. Soon they found themselves in front of a house, sprawling, beautiful and aesthetically built, with a lawn spread over a few acres. The young man gaped at it for a moment and then he read aloud, 'Advocate Ranjit Singh.' His father had smiled. He decided to go inside and talk to Advocate Ranjit Singh.

'The initial years are tough,' Advocate Ranjit Singh was telling him, maybe that explained the presence of *Das Capital* on his book shelves, maybe those days, a bungalow-less, a lawn-less Advocate Ranjit Singh drew solace from the writings of Karl Marx. Anyhow, those days were different. No mad rush to acquire more and more. No boom in consumerism. When poverty was looked upon with respect, when one followed the Biblical philosophy, it is as easy for the rich to enter the gates of heaven as it is for the camel to pass through the needle's eye. Advocate Ranjit Singh belonged to that age. When Nehruvian ideals of secularism and socialism held the ground

Yet Advocate Ranjit Singh managed to earn a lot. And he did not mind earning. Karl Marx notwithstanding. If rumours are to be believed, half of Bulandshahar belonged to Advocate Ranjit Singh.

'Son, when I started I had a *chowki* and a *lota.* Now the rest is for you to see,' Advocate Ranjit Singh was smiling, a slight smile, one that played on his lips every time he won a case.

'There are many who, at the end, are not able to retain even the *chowki* and the *lota',* he added.

The young man gave a long, intent look to Advocate Ranjit Singh. And then he rose, a grim determination on his face, his hands folded behind him.

'Thank you, sir,' he said, his eyes gleaming. He left the room, shutting the door quietly behind him.

Advocate Ranjit Singh smiled. Suddenly he felt young. Young like the man who had left his room a few minutes back.

Lola's Kunti Chachi

The women had gathered in the courtyard for singing and dancing, one of the essential rituals of the wedding. They saw Kunti coming towards them, her *saree* rolled and shortened to knee length, her lips painted garishly with red lipstick. 'Sing, sing', she urged the others but everyone was silent, none daring to open mouth now that Kunti was there. She caught hold of a plate and a spoon, a big spoon made of brass, and handing it over to her little neighbour, she started dancing in full swing.

'How paradoxical!' *Chhoti Chachi* exclaimed, 'Montu does not care for her, he does not come to see her even once a year, but see the enthusiasm of his wife!' Kunti, in the meanwhile, oblivious of all this, was in the middle of the courtyard, her head covered, her legs exposed till her knees, her face brimming with enthusiasm, bending and clapping, bending and clapping. The others joined her but none could match her speed. I could faintly hear the women in the courtyard and wanted very much to be a part of the festivities, but Lola was sleepy and she had to be fed and made to go off to sleep. It is so irritating but Lola would be cranky at this hour only, at around eight o'clock, when the ladies of the locality would start collecting, Chintu would be ready with his camera, the older men and women would bring their chairs to sit in the verandah, and watch the women celebrate. And then, as if on a cue, Lola would start crying.

I saw Kunti for the first time when I went to attend Tinku's wedding, though I had heard a lot about her. We had a great time discussing her, on the dining table, when we had finished with our meal and wanted something juicy, something spicy, to discuss and liven our conversation with. None else but Kunti would come to our rescue on these occasions. 'Yesterday Kunti beat up *Badi Chachi* so ruthlessly! Had *Chhote Chacha* not intervened, she would have fractured her legs!' By then Lola had finished eating, and also, I was highly interested; when? where? how? I wanted to ask hundreds of questions at the same time. Had it been a story of a mother-in-law beating the daughter-in-law or, maybe, a husband beating a wife, I would not have been so interested. Here there was something different. Something fascinating. Just the right kind of dessert after dinner. Had it not been for the bruises and the near fracture of bones which *Badi Chachi* and others suffered at her hand, I would have called it humorous. I was known for cracking jokes on wives beating their husbands but this was not a joke. But why does not Montu go to his wife? I was curious. Why has he abandoned his daughter? It reminded me of my own Lola. And then another story would begin, the story of Montu and the other woman.

Well. There was this man called Montu. Our own Montu. By the age of twenty-five all his friends were married and there was no reason why he should also not marry. So he married with great pomp and show. His house was illuminated with series of bulbs, those small bulbs that blinked and were hired during weddings, crackers were burst, he was attired in a silk *dhoti* and a matching silk *kurta* and then he was sent to fetch his bride. His brand new bride. Our own Kunti. In the beginning Kunti was pampered by the folks in the family and there was no reason why Montu would also not pamper her. They lived in a joint family, ate in commensality, gossiped and did the other things together. This is not to say things were all sweet and rosy and that there were no fights and quarrels as is normal in any household. *Badi Chachi* taunted Kunti because she could not bring as much gold as was expected of her, or as her father had promised, nor was she as fair as had been suggested (it being a conservative family, Montu was allowed to get a glimpse of her in a photograph and satisfy himself with that). Not that Kunti was all sweet and sugar for she more than took her revenge by mimicking and backbiting. But then this was normal. What was not normal was what was to take place later; after Montu had acquired a job in Calcutta.

The job in Calcutta was rewarding and Montu liked it. The house at Calcutta was to his liking, and the landlady, more so. The landlady had a very sad story to tell and Montu was never bored. He would be all ears every time she would begin. How her husband beat her up in public, at times dragging her by her hair while her children watched, frightened, shivering, he did not give any food to her and her children for several days, he did not buy anything for her. So moved was Montu by this pathetic story that he immediately went to his village, by the very next bus, collected all the jewellery of Kunti, while she was dreaming, and handed it over to the tortured woman. So while one woman, the tortured one, was loaded with jewellery, the other who slept was robbed of whatever she had.

Then Kunti started beating *Badi Chachi*. She would throw utensils, made of brass, steel and aluminium, slippers that Montu had bought for her years back and which now bore marks of frequent repair, her daughter's toys, anything she could lay her hands on. Suddenly, in the dead of night, everyone would be awakened by *Badi Chachi's* screams and they would all run..... the filthy abuse that emanated from the room mingled with the screams of the old lady while they tried to bring things in control. So terrified would the old matron be that she would rather sleep with *Chhoti Chachi, or Anju Didi, or Manju Didi* that night, the taste of being beaten up fresh in her mind. 'This woman is responsible for my plight', Kunti would yell, 'she assisted her son in running away, she will have to pay for it; where are you hiding, you old hag?' *Badi Chachi* did not have the guts to respond, feeling safe and secure in her sister-in-law's room. After an hour or so, when she thought Kunti had gone off to sleep, she left her room stealthily, and peeped into the room where her daughter-in-law was sleeping. It seems Kunti was waiting for her. 'Come, Come,' she gestured, 'I think you are not satisfied yet, I think you need some more.' The old woman ran away, Kunti laughing all the while, her teeth flashing demon-like.

So, as I mentioned earlier, I saw Kunti for the first time when I went to the village to attend Tinku's wedding. *Didi* nudged at me and pointed towards a thin lady who had limped into the room; she was wearing no slippers, the soles of her feet were cracked like parched earth. She had applied a lot of talcum powder on her face, her painted lips looked garish, almost obscene. The moment my eyes fell on her I knew it was she. I introduced myself which she acknowledged with a smile. *'Chhotki Bahuriya?'*

'Yes,' I stood up and adjusted myself on the bed to give her some place to sit. She took an instant liking to Lola. 'Lola, come with me, I will show you a goat,' she had come to know that Lola, like other children of her age, was very fond of animals, black buffalo, white cow, brown cow, white and brown goat, black goat, and she intended to win the little child's heart by showing her what she liked the best. In a moment Kunti had disappeared with the child. I was worried. One cannot trust her, going by the track record she has. But I was wrong, she was very gentle with the child, gentle as velvet, may be because she was a mother and had a mother's heart. Maybe she was seeing the reflection of her own daughter in my child.

Her daughter did not live with her. Montu had stopped providing even the subsistence allowance which she received earlier; after all it was not so easy to support two families, his Calcutta family consisted of a woman and her six children. Like a dutiful man, he endeavoured to satisfy the needs of this family, while his first wife and her child were left alone to fend for themselves. So Kunti left her daughter with her mother at Luklukki and survived by eating whatever her mother-in-law gave her, periodically beating her and blaming her for her pitiable condition. Once I asked Kunti why she did not go to the doctor and got herself cured of her limp. 'Will you give money for this? I will go today itself,' she challenged. I had no answer.

A few days back, when we were having our tea on the terrace, with Lola prancing around like the monkey she loved, and her grandfather playing with her, I was told about Kunti. That *Badi Chachi* had left the house where Kunti terrorised her and she went to Calcutta, to her new daughter-in-law, her son's latest choice. Very juicy. I was all ears. 'S-h-a-m-e a-n-d s-c-a-n-d-a-l i-n t-h-e f-a-m-i-l-y......,' I started humming. I had always liked it. It was only that this time I was feeling a bit bad. Almost guilty. 'So things must be easy for *Badi Chachi* now,' I sounded concerned. 'Yes, of course,' I was told, 'the new woman takes care of her, attending to all her needs.' Thankfully *Chachi* can now have some peace. A sigh. But what about Kunti? She goes to the others' houses in search of food.

'Why don't you go to your mother?' she was asked one day, 'after all your daughter is also there!'

'And leave Montu to do whatever he wishes to!' she shot back, 'I will never leave his house. I know he does not have the guts to kick me out, my h-u-s-b-a-n-d,' she was chewing every word.

Montu really did not have the guts.

I think I should end the story now for I am in a hurry. I have to finish with the chores before Lola comes back from her school. We have put her in a play school, about half a kilometer from our apartment, where she goes every day, with a bag, a lunch box and a red water bottle, bright as fresh tomato. Lola does not remember Kunti *Chachi* though she does remember the black and white goat she had played with. Well, let me go back to Kunti. One day she did go to her husband to plead with him to come back. She was refused entry. But Kunti was undeterred, she refused to budge till she saw Montu. Anyway, Montu was tipped off and he managed to escape before Kunti could find him. Kunti returned.

I hear their daughter has grown up. The mother wants the jewellery back so that she can marry her off. I am amazed. I am amazed because Kunti still refuses to go back to her mother at Luklukki. I am amazed because her husband has never felt like seeing his daughter, now grown up, in this span of ten years. I am amazed because the house in which Kunti still lives resounds with her filthy abuse while no one dares to stop her. Everyone is frightened of her including her husband. They have had a child, and Montu is nowadays busy taking care of their new born baby. He had celebrated her naming ceremony with great fanfare, inviting practically everyone from the village. Except for Kunti and her daughter. Well. This does not amaze me. For a change.

Mistaken Identity

He was stripped of his clothes and beaten mercilessly. He kept howling in pain but all his entreaties fell on deaf ears. '*Amma, Amma*', he continued wailing till he fell unconscious. Flies swarmed around the blood that had clotted on his forehead, on the left hand side. The knuckles of his fingers were broken, and his face was disfigured beyond recognition. 'Bastard!' the policeman swore, unable to make him confess to anything.

The policeman flopped on the chair, tired. He ordered a cup of tea and drank it noisily. Occasionally he raised his right arm, curled all his fingers, so that they resembled a hooded cobra, and then tried trapping the flies in that cave-like thing. He would then rub the flies between two of his fingers, the flattened bodies he looked upon with a sense of satisfaction. The policeman looked at him through the iron bars; he was half naked, half unconscious.

He remembered waking up in the morning and taking his bicycle to fetch milk from the local dairy. He had fought with his sister that day. But what was his fault? He had simply asked her to prepare a cup of tea with lots of sugar and she stuck out her tongue, teasing him, and said there was no sugar. Infuriated, he ran to the kitchen, picked up the jar of sugar and flung it at her. She simply laughed and ran away. Anyway, there was nothing new in all this, he turned his bicycle towards the booth and smiled. He could discern the figure of Ramesh approaching. Ramesh and other boys in the locality, would gather around the milk booth every morning and after collecting milk, the whole group would sit, smoke a few cigarettes and then decide what to do after attending the college. 'They are showing a good movie in *Shakuntalam* today,' Ramesh chirped, 'why don't we miss classes today and watch the first show!'

'No, no,' Deepu, his friend, had his reservations, 'if Papa comes to know of it, he will be very angry with me.'

'C'mon, be a man!' all of them jeered at him and finally they all agreed to go for the show that day.

He had borrowed Deepu's motorcycle and had reached *Shakuntalam* exactly fifteen minutes before time; Ramesh had already bought the tickets, later on they would sit and decide who has to pay how much. He had lighted a cigarette and watched with avid interest the flock of girls that had come from the nearby college, *Venkateshwara*, to watch the movie. The girl in pink captivated him- very fair, she dimpled when she smiled. He had winked at her. She glared at him and disappeared in the crowd.

Later on, at night, when he was taking his dinner, *idli* with thick *sambhar*, his father cracked a joke,

'A man told his wife, "Look, I love your relatives more than those of mine."

'Any proof?'

'Yes, of course! Don't I love your mother-in-law more than mine?'

Somebody had rung the bell. They were surprised. Who can come at this time? He opened the door and saw two men in *khaki*. 'Whose motorcycle is this?' they were pointing towards Deepu's motorcycle he had parked in front of the house, a piece of cloth thrown over it for protection from dust and rain. 'It is my friend's, I had borrowed it from him today,' he answered. He was frightened, he did not know what the matter was. 'You will have to come to the police station for certain enquiries,' one of them had said, the same man who had ordered he be thrashed later on, both his legs on the table, his eyes oozing blood.

'But what is the matter?' his father intervened.

'Nothing. We will only ask him a few questions', the policeman had said, in a matter of fact manner, his face expressionless.

He was kept in police lockup for two hours without being told anything. At around eleven o'clock, four men in uniform entered his cell, immediately followed by the fifth one, one who sounded like their superior. 'Where are the rest of them?' the superior enquired. He looked at them, stunned. 'Where are the others? Where did you get the bomb from? Who is behind all this? Who is your leader?'

Now he was really frightened. 'Please leave me, I do not know anything,' he was terrified.

He saw that one of them had already lifted his hand to strike him. He was struck on his lower elbow with such force that for a moment he could see everything dance before his eyes. Now they had started kicking him, slapping him, hitting him at all places. He had never felt such excruciating pain before. One of them, a fat man with double chin, took out his belt and lashed out at him. 'Tch, tch,' he chuckled, 'look at the innocence on his face; who would say he is such a big rogue?' Now he was howling in pain, licking his own blood that had trickled down from his forehead. He clutched at his stomach, trying to protect himself desperately. Boom Boom Boom. Now they had tied his hands behind him. Unable to bear it any longer, he collapsed.

'Are you certain he is one of them?' he could faintly hear someone, peeping at him, trying to sprinkle water on his face to bring him to senses.

'Yes, yes, it is the same motorcycle on which they had come- DLA 6345.'

The ordeal continued. One of them stooped and pulled the undergarment from his body. He shrieked. He did not know where to hide his face. He could hear his own bones smash like the broken glass tumbler. He remembered having fractured his toe once while playing football. His friends panicked and he was immediately taken to the hospital. And his mother. ... She refused to budge from the hospital till he was discharged. The whole day she sat near him, crying all the time and pleading with him to stop playing football. Where is his mother now? '*Amma, Amma,*' he moaned. But his mother did not come. Instead, the men in *khaki* reappeared.

He lay there, motionless, wondering what would come next. To his surprise, no one was kicking at him this time. Instead, one of them motioned towards him to get up and wear his clothes. He made an effort to get up, tottered, and then started dressing up slowly, fearing what was to follow next.

'Sorry! It was a case of mistaken identity,' one of them mumbled, 'you may go now.'

On reaching home, he knocked at the door. His sister shrieked when she saw him standing there. He started limping towards his bedroom, holding his sister's arm for support.

He has never left his house after that.

'Shh!' putting his finger on his lips, he would say, 'talk softly, the men in *khaki* are standing outside! If they hear us, they will not spare me this time!'

Vermilion And The Yellow Saree

The Medical Report said, she was not a virgin. Her age was 16-17 years.

She had not left her house after the incident. In fact, once about two to three days back, when she had to visit the lady doctor, she was accompanied by her brother who held her wrist so tight that it hurt. Her heart also ached though she mentioned this to no one. When her friend Malti came to see her, she felt sad. The dark room where she had imprisoned herself had a ghost-like feeling; the room had small windows with vertical bars, and a spring for the curtains to hang. Discoloured, gloomy. The first thing that Malti did on entering her room was to open the windows when fresh air rushed inside; this made her shiver. Bright light and fresh air terrified her. The solitude of her room filled her with a sense of security.

The tutor had been coming to their house everyday for giving tuition to her sister and her. Her sister was only ten. Though she was growing up.

So he was her teacher, in a sense. Once *Bhaiji*, her cousin, had tried to rove into her private parts. Though at her age she could not comprehend what was happening, she knew something was terribly wrong somewhere. Every time she turned, he paused, he held his breath. The moment she fell into a slumber, his fingers started moving again. In the morning when she woke up, she could recollect what had happened during the night. Though she could not exactly pinpoint where the problem lay, her instinct compelled her not to mention this to anyone. Not even to Malti. And she remembered feeling quite dirty throughout the day. Though she had bathed twice that day, the soap having been completely flattened, the dirty feeling did not go.

The tutor gave lessons to them thrice a week; she invariably served tea to him during winters, when he came on a motorcycle, wearing a high-neck sweater of three colours, the three colours used to knit three lines criss-crossing one another. During summers she would serve him *sherbet* in a tall, steel glass with a polished exterior. At times she could see her face, reflected in the glass, compressed and sometimes broadened. When she handed over the glass of *sherbet* to him, she felt his fingers brush the palm of her hand. She felt her heart pound and she would find it difficult to comprehend whatever he taught her after that. She raised her eyes to look at him and this did not help matters.

Seven days and seven nights. She had stayed with the man who had given her tuition. In a small room six by six. The developed breasts that the doctor had mentioned in her report were touched and re-touched a million times. Nights filled her with dread and also gave her pleasure. This time she liked it; though she had not liked *Bhaiji's* roving hands.

Pandit Deenanath, her father, one who had a sallow face and coloured teeth, had lodged a report with the police. The elderly neighbour informed that he had seen his daughter with her tutor around seven o'clock, when a man can still be recognized with a naked eye, without the aid of a lantern. In fact, he was certain that he had seen Pandit Deenanath's daughter with her tutor, on the latter's motorcycle, one hand encircling the tutor's waist. 'Govind's *Ma'*, he remembered telling his wife shortly afterward, taking out his plastic shoes at the entrance of his house, '*Panditji* should be more careful with his daughter.'

'Why, what has happened?' *Panditji's* wife was puzzled.

'I don't like her ways,' he walked away muttering, the bristles on his head, freshly shaven, stood like nails on a wooden board.

She knew *Baba* had seen her. She also knew that Chinta *Chachi* and Jhunni had seen her. But she wanted to go with her tutor to see a movie in the theatre. The tutor said he would buy the tickets and then they could sit and enjoy the movie in the dark hall. She could feel the crawling fingers of the tutor in the darkness.

She stated before the Judicial Magistrate that she had been taken forcibly by him. She had said, 'he said, "I will shoot you" when I had offered resistance.'

Not for once was she frightened when she went with the tutor. Both of them boarded a train, after that they had watched a movie and took their meal at a wayside eatery. She snuggled close to him, his body giving her warmth. She had smiled at a child staring at them. The child had some *golis* which he had placed on his outstretched palm; he extended his hand and offered her *golis*, blackish grey in colour. She picked up two, ate one and offered the other to the tutor. The *goli* dissolved in her mouth. She licked her lips to savour the taste, small fragments that had deposited on her lips were again licked with a rolling tongue.

The tutor took her to a small room. The entrance was dirty, with open, stinking drain, that bordered the narrow lane leading up to the room. She knew she should not have come with her tutor; she felt his smouldering eyes on her. She adjusted her *dupatta*.

Night after night passed. The tutor had taken her to a temple and smeared vermilion on the parting of her hair. Though she was habituated to parting her hair sideways, that day she had taken care to part her hair in the middle. The vermilion shone and looked like a bloody strip painted with water colour.

They stayed together for a few days, unrecognized by anyone. No one knew them in the city they had come to.

One day they decided to return. The tutor said he would take her to his village. Though she did not receive a warm welcome in her new home, the essential rituals of welcoming the new bride were performed. The tutor's sister had remarked, 'the girl has such a flat nose, what did my brother see in this ugly duckling?' Though her reception was lukewarm, she was allowed to participate in household activities. The tutor's father was a stern man, he harangued his son. His mother counted on her fingers the marriage proposals they had received for their son, with fabulous offers of dowry along with the bride. She was shown some photographs, black and white passport size photographs; all the girls sat on a stool with their hands placed on their thighs in a particular way. The tutor's mother had preserved them like trophies.

Her father, *Panditji,* had lodged a complaint with the police. The police had been able to recover her from the tutor's house. 'She is my wife,' the tutor claimed, pointing towards the vermilion on her parting.

'We shall see that in the police station,' the man in *khaki* said.

She had dreamt of her tutor that night. The tutor was a Rajput and she a Brahmin. In her dream she saw that the tutor was standing with his hands folded, his lower lip moving. He said, 'they made me drink a bottle of liquor and then they beat me the whole night.'

She woke up, terrified. She poured a glass of water from the jug she normally kept on the stool near her bed. She had three glasses of water. Then she carefully placed the glass on the jug, facing downward, the drops of water remaining in the glass making a circular ring. She looked out of the window through the mosquito net she had hung with the help of strings which she had then fastened on to the nails that had been hammered into the four walls. It was quiet outside. Occasionally a dog barked, breaking the peace that had existed. Then it was again quiet. It contrasted with the storm that was raging in her heart.

The tutor's sister had visited her in the morning. She had said they had been very harsh with her brother in police custody. *Panditji* had bribed them, she knew. He limps. He walks with difficulty. His sister went back, pleading mercy.

She drank another glass of water. Cold drops fell on her throat, giving her a burning sensation. She let the drops ooze into her *kurta,* making a wet patch near her neck. Then she took her *dupatta* and began fanning herself, the mosquitoes that had sneaked in through the hole in the net were moving noisily. She raised her hands, aimed at a mosquito, and then joined them together, crushing the winged creature. There was blood on her hands, she could see, it lay there, stuck to her palm, flattened and bloodied.

She did not like going to the court. People looked at her in strange ways. She had seen a man from her village outside the court precincts, he gestured towards her and spat. She felt the spit clang to her body.

The defence counsel looked at her and asked her several questions. She replied to all his questions. The tutor was also present in the courtroom.

She repeated the whole story, in bits and pieces, like the pieces in the jigsaw puzzle, which were then placed in the correct slots. It sounded convincing to her own ears, she was surprised. She found the tutor seeing her furiously, she averted her eyes. She did not know he would become a stranger to her so soon. 'He is given coarse *rotis* in the jail,' his sister was wailing, 'my brother is so fond of eating, he gets food fit for animals.'

'Even the animals get a better treatment.' Dinu joined in, 'When I went to Patna zoo, with my granddaughter Sheelu, I was pleasantly surprised to see the kind of treatment the animals get from the authorities.'

'Men huddled in small corners like cows and buffaloes.'

She had also heard the snatches of conversation. Her heart ached. She had not exactly disliked being with the tutor; though going to watch the movie was not exactly her idea. She was unaware of his plans of taking the train later on. Still, she had not protested. When the tutor had smeared vermilion on her parting and they exchanged garlands, she had liked it; she was party to it, but her father, Pandit Deenanath, would kill her if she said so. So she repeated before the defence counsel, 'He said, "I will shoot you," if I refused to accompany him.'

The tutor was good-looking. He was wearing black trousers with a full sleeve shirt that had black and white stripes. She had heard him park his motorcycle outside the gate of her house, under the mango tree. Her heart beat fast. The tutor ignored his sister who was trying to attract his attention to get a mathematical sum solved. Sixteen multiplied by eight and divided by two. Two was then added to the result. Her sister's calculation was wrong somewhere. Her answer was not matching with the answer given at the end, where the answers were given chapter-wise. Each chapter contained about ten to twelve answers to the questions given. But the tutor knew that he had to help out her sister. He sat down, looking at the calculations done in pencil, rubbed at several places and rewritten, the mark of the original writing still visible. He did the calculation mentally, his answer did not match with the one given at the back. He took the pencil and made the calculations in the copybook, this time also he met with no success. He was getting impatient. She entered the room, balancing the tray with the tutor's tea with one hand and holding the curtain with the other. The tutor got up, took his tea, and started sipping it noisily. Her eyes met his. He smiled. Then he finished with his tea, placed the cup on the tray that was on the study table, with their books and copybooks. At times it was difficult to say which books belonged to her and which to her sister. They looked alike when covered with newspaper. Both the sisters also looked alike, wearing the same kind of clothes. Her mother bought long pieces of cloth from the market and she stitched similar dresses for both of them, from the same piece of cloth. She knew the tutor liked her. Teaching her gave him pleasure but with her sister he seemed to be fulfilling some duty. As if he was trying to justify the tuition fee he received from Pandit Deenanath every month.

On the first of every month, Pandit Deenanath invariably entered the room where they sat and studied, holding his *dhoti* and the cash amount, when the tutor rose to touch his feet. Her father would then raise his hand to bless him, after which he would point towards the chair, indicating that the tutor should sit down. After that Pandit Deenanath would discuss the progress of the girls' education, the mere mention of her name bringing a glow to the tutor's face, which the old man's eyes could not discern. Pandit Deenanath would then rise, holding the upper part of the chair for support, and say, 'Work hard. Take his help.' And when all this was over, they would resume their studies. This was repeated month after month.

One day she saw the tutor in the courtroom and she did not recognize him. There were bristles on his cheeks; he had not shaved. Except for that, of course, he had not changed much. Same defiant looks, same eyes that smouldered when they fell on her.

The tutor's mother had sent a set of bangles, vermilion, and a white *saree* dyed in yellow. She knew it was the custom to send yellow *sarees* after marriage. The tutor's sister had come to her neighbour's house the day before and had gone back saying, 'Ma wants my sister-in-law to wear these tomorrow on *Batsavitri*.' *Batsavitri*. As the legend goes, Savitri, the dutiful wife, snatched Satyavan, her husband, from the claws of death. So on *Batsavitri*, the day on which Savitri rescued her husband, all the married women prayed for their husbands' lives and fasted for their welfare. The *saree* dyed in yellow and the bangles were in her neighbour's hands. She looked at her face and said nothing. Handing over the things her neighbour had hidden in her black bag, to avoid detection, she left her room saying, 'Do what you think is best for you.'

It was dark. Everyone had gone off to sleep. She had hung her mosquito net on the four nails in the four corners. It was so quiet she could hear her own heartbeat. She took out the *saree* and wore it, the bangles were then worn with care. The vermilion sent by her tutor's mother was applied on the parting. After that, she muttered, *'Masterji, Masterji'* and then shut her eyes. The tutor, it seemed, was standing in front of her, smiling.

When she got up the next day, early in the morning, her eyes fell on the *saree* and the golden bangles she wore. She looked out of the window, the sky dark with black clouds, hanging like passengers on a crowded bus. Then she got up with a jerk. Pandit Deenanath was sitting in the courtyard, her anklets made *chan chan chan* sound, as she came near him. He raised his head, the expression on his face started changing slowly but distinctly, as she started speaking.

'*Babuji*, I am leaving your house. Forgive me my follies, and let me go now,' saying so she touched Pandit Deenanath's feet, who hastened to pull them away from her.

She started walking towards the village of her tutor.

The Fugitive Family

Back home they had a big house, a car and two lovely children. Now they live in a small two-bedroom apartment, matchbox kind of a thing, they would say, as big as the servant's quarter in their home in the valley. They were not exactly millionaires but they had more than sufficient. 'Rich enough,' the wife would say, 'and a relaxed life.'

They are glued to their TV set, munching chips, absorbing every bit of information they are getting, reporters giving an hourly update on the bombings in the small, impoverished mountain state. The land where they were born, Kashmir, has once again become a hot topic. A reporter came from a local English newspaper in the morning, after an appointment.

'What was it like?' he was asking, poised with a sheet of paper and a ballpoint.

The wife began, her eyes acquiring a strange expression, 'They, in short, ruined our lives.'

The husband continued, 'They were four of them, their faces wrapped up in black clothes. I could hear a few gunshots. "Go, see what the problem is", my wife urged. Probably I was the only one who came out, or may be, being a Hindu Brahmin, I was their real target; one of them saw me and fired, inflicting a wound on my left hand. I ran inside, holding the hand that bled profusely, shouting and directing my four-year son to get inside, for I had seen him peeping from the window of his room........'

The wife ran inside.

They were bombarding Afghanistan, the mountain state. A small child was shown on TV, hysterical. His mother was telling how he started trembling everyday, as a matter of routine, as the sun set, darkness raised its head like the serpent. The Big Boss undertook its daily ritual of bombardment. The child shivered all night, the sound of the bombs making him sit up and cling to his mother. The mother thought of leaving. But where to go? Cartloads of men and women were fleeing to the border area. Her brother had also attempted the same. They all sat on the cart, loaded with pots and pans and clothes, the cart wobbling like an old man with a funny gait. They were all silenced as a bomb hit them, reducing them and their cart to ashes.

The wife came back with a half sleeve shirt and a pair of white shorts with black stripes. With dark maroon stains, which now looked almost blackish. They had come inside the house, following the father, breaking the pot containing a big, white dahlia. They had seen the boy, his eyes resting on the iron bars of the window, one of the fingernails painted blue, the other green. They caught him from behind, the unsuspecting boy letting out a hoarse cry.

'Maaaaaaaaaaaaaaa!'

They were carrying sharp edged weapons, the kind he saw the butchers use when they cut the animals for human consumption. They dragged the boy by his collar, bringing him to the central lobby. 'So there, right in front of us, they cut our boy's head. *Halal* !'

'Let this be an example,' they yelled, 'leave our land, you idol worshippers!'

The man from the desert is a dreaded man. Highly admired by some. Likewise, highly hated by some. 'Just get that bastard,' seems to be the mood in the country of abundance right now. God may forgive them, we will not.

'Please don't attack us,' says the impoverished state, once known for dry fruits and now for Bamiyan Buddhas.

'Alright, but hand over the man from the desert to us.'

'No way!' the *Mullah* is defiant.

The war has begun.

The dusk has fallen and the boy has started shivering. He does not know who the man from the desert is but he does know about his uncle who was killed by the bomb for which this man from the desert was responsible. His cousins, who died with this uncle, as they were trying to wobble to safety, were his friends. The sound of the bomb filled him with terror.

'The situation is tense in the Valley,' the TV announces. The journalist with the sheet and the ballpoint feels like having a glass of water. They are showing mangled bodies, limbs thrown yards away from the torso, the faces disfigured. The wife is weeping. She had seen her own son being butchered in front of her. The sight of mangled bodies, strewn on the road, vermilion-red blood dripping like ice cream, fills her with nausea.

The husband understands. He signals to the daughter to get up and switch off the TV. The wife is holding her head, the shirt with half sleeve and the shorts with black stripes have been thrown on the sofa. Now they have only one child, a daughter. She is taking computer classes, asking her parents to forget the past. She has never gone to the Valley after that nocturnal flight. Here she lives in a small two-room apartment while their palatial house is now occupied by the men with black mask.

The child with innocent gaping eyes still shivers with the fall of dusk. 'Why do they want to kill us?' he asks his father.

'Because we have given shelter to a man they want,' the father replies.

'Where have you hid him? In the room at the extreme corner, where we hoard our grains? That explains why you always lock it up,' the boy concluded. The father was silent.

'One of my friends is lying in the hospital,' he suddenly panicked, 'both his legs have been badly damaged by the bomb. *Abbu,* for heaven's sake, when will all this stop?'

In reply, his father let out a sigh.

Establishing themselves in Delhi was not easy for the fugitive family. No car, no house. Delhi was hot. The wife somehow managed to get a job of a receptionist in Mehrauli, she had to spend four hours travelling to and fro. Add to it additional seven to eight hours she spent in the office, receiving calls, transferring them, and working on the PC at the same time, and you know what it is like.

The husband stayed at home, looked after the daughter, and bought the vegetables from a market held near their house. Once he felt like buying a plastic ball for his headless son back home and he did buy one, placing it next to the shorts and shirt his wife had kept in the cupboard. His wife came back late at night, saw the ball kept next to the shirt and shorts, cooked dinner and went off to sleep without eating. She did not go to the office for next few days. The husband panicked, what will happen if she loses her job? How will they subsist? Thankfully the wife recovered soon, her employer understood, but the husband was more careful after that.

Once the daughter was playing in the park with her friends, one of them Bilal. Hide and seek. She was blindfolded and supposed to catch either one of her friends and then, she was to guess the name of the captive. She caught Bilal, instantly recognizing him by the smell of the perfume he wore, and pinned him to the ground. 'Chop off his neck, I've caught him !' she shouted, shuddering all the while. 'They killed my brother, we will kill him. We are more here!' A triumphant smile played on her lips. They had great difficulty in extricating Bilal's hair from her fist, tightly shut. Bilal never came to play with them after the incident. He had new friends.

Now the daughter has to be married off. They need money. They have certainly come a long way from a one-room accommodation to a two bed-room apartment. With a kitchen, with woodwork, a bathroom with marble floor and white tiles on the walls, an extended balcony with pots of plants. Two air-conditioners, fitted in both the bedrooms, making Delhi much more pleasant. But still they yearn for their home in the Valley.

The boy in the mountain state knows his friend in the hospital has to have both his feet amputated. It is tragic. He is sitting on the rooftop, shirtless, shoeless.

The woman from the Valley did not like her job in the beginning. With a son lost and a hard life, she cursed those bearded men. Anyway, after two years the husband managed to get a job, the office situated 10 km from where they stayed, hardly any distance considering the kind of distances in Delhi. The wife was too happy to do what she did earlier, cooking and cleaning.

The Big Boss was saying, 'Terrorism is a global problem, we shall uproot it.'

'We shall fight till the end,' he added.

The world is angry. Eye for an eye. Tooth for a tooth. Hammurabi's principle still holding good. The Big Boss did not know it was so vulnerable.

The fugitive family from the Valley does not lose hope. The vendor came cycling, rolled the newspaper, put a black rubber band on it, and then aimed at the balcony. It hit the husband right on his head, almost spilling *kahwa* that he had in his balcony everyday in the morning. Unrolling the newspaper, and spreading it on the cane chair- it had become wet as it fell on water that had collected in the balcony, it had rained heavily the previous night, the sky had been black with clouds- the husband gave a furtive glance. Something held his attention for a moment. He smiled. It was a broad smile. He had never been this happy ever since he had seen his son's *halal*. The husband read:

'Bilal, a boy aged twenty-four, known for his extremist views, was found dead in the fields adjoining Tripti Apartment, Sector VI, Noida. It is suspected that men from a certain community are responsible for his killing. He was beheaded, the head lying close to his body, and all his fingers were cut. The case is being investigated.'

The Big Boss continues to bombard the mountain state, the fugitive from the desert is still elusive, the world has become Bilal-less and the headless boy from the Valley continues to haunt his mother.

The Fighter

Somya was the eldest child in the family. Minku, her younger brother, was my contemporary, we studied in the same school. Slightly spoilt, he never lost an opportunity to take advantage of the fact that his mother was our school principal whom we held in great esteem. Somya was dark but attractive. There was something in her face that men found difficult to resist. I was not close to Somya but I would meet her on Sundays when I went to their house to watch a movie on their television. Somya's parents were one of the first ones in the locality to acquire a TV set. All of us made a beeline to Somya's house, on Sunday evenings, where her mother gave us *chuda,* flattened rice, in steel bowls, with small spoons; we munched our *chuda* while watching song and dance sequences.

At times I went to play with Minku. They had a small *puja* room where they had placed some idols of Lord Shiva and Parvati; it was here that I would go with Minku and perform a mock *puja.* Minku would bring an incense stick and a box of matches, and we would light the brass lamp, and mutter, with great devotion, *'Jai Ganesh, Jai Ganesh, Jai Ganesh Deva,'* with our eyes shut the way we had seen our elders do. Children are monkeys, they will try repeating anything they see. Dara, their father, would, at times, ruffle my hair fondly; he was very fond of us. Once he said, 'My child, tell your father I want to know who he is voting for in the elections.' My father told me he would talk to Minku's father about it.

Somya had a sharp tongue. Her mother was a Malyalee, who, even after years of marriage with a North Indian, had a poor knowledge of Hindi. Somya, when angry, would rattle a string of abuses at her Malyalee mother who did not understand what her daughter said; she, of course, understood, what her daughter said was certainly not complimentary. She would tell her elder son Pinku, 'write down, write down, whatever she says. When Dara comes home, we will show it to him.' Pinku, the dutiful son, would take a sheet and a pen and write what Somya had said. At times he would add some words on his own to make the reading more colourful.

Somya's mother particularly disliked some of the alliances she was making with the boys of the locality. A local bully, Tanee, had moustaches that made us, young children, frightened. He had the eyes that threatened to kill whomsoever he decided to. Somya frequented Tanee's place quite often. We children never dared to ask about Tanee but the day we had gone to river *Ganga* for the holy bath, on *Chath*, the festival of Sun God, we saw Tanee. To me, he looked like a demon, bathed in early morning sunlight. Their relationship was much talked about, in the days to come, especially by Lalli's sister and my sister. Lalli was my neighbour and classmate, we shared our tiffins and our little secrets. Later on, we were in the same college, attending the same tutorials when Rekha, her elder sister, threatened to rag us and we smiled at her. We had smiled when Rekha and my elder sister talked of Somya and when we tried to eavesdrop, Rekha had rebuked us. But Somya continued to be a kind of mystery to us. There was a veil around her which we could never penetrate, try as we did.

Then Somya fell in love with Manik, a friend of Tanee and his gang. Manik's mother, a woman of high caste and very refined, tried hard to dissuade her son from having anything to do with Somya. Manik did not listen to his mother. We heard Somya fastened a shoe to the bamboo stick, and when Manik's mother was in her balcony, Somya unfastened the shoe and pointed it at Manik's mother. A woman of fine sensibility, Manik's mother found Somya's conduct revolting and uncouth. The day Manik conveyed his decision to marry Somya, his mother did not perform *puja*.

'If God does not listen to my prayers, why should I bow before him every day?' she told her elder daughter-in-law, my cousin.

Somya was pregnant. Manik and Somya had taken a one-room set on rent, far away from where their parents lived. The maidservant who went to massage Somya came back with stories which the entire neighbourhood lapped up with interest. 'You see,' she would say, 'whenever I enter her room, Tanee Fanee, and all the others, I find, sitting there.' The women would want to hear more. 'If the men want to leave,' the maid is enjoying the attention she is receiving, ' Somya asks them not to, and asks me to do my work there and then.'

'Did you expose her buttocks for oil massage?' a curious woman asked.

'Yes, yes,' the maid obliged, 'while they all sat there.'

Stories kept trickling in, like the rays of sun stealing into the dark room through a small hole, and the women would cajole the maid to tell them more as to what was happening at Somya's place, particularly if it was salacious.

When Somya's first child, a daughter, was born, we all went to her place for her *chhathi,* the auspicious sixth day of the birth of the child. On first five days, the child wears old clothes, the clothes that are passed on by the older children of the family. We had gone with a frock and a nappy set and an oblong toy that made a lot of noise when moved to and fro. Somya's mother had brought hand sewn nappies and baby mattresses, a washable quilt, white as lime, which had a red and blue mickey mouse embroidered on it. And, other gifts. There was some gold and silver also. Manik's parents did not come to her son's place that day. We understood why.

Then my cousin got married to Manik's elder brother, a fresh graduate from Bangalore Engineering College, down south. When unmarried, he could be found occasionally on his rooftop, adjoining ours, wearing white shirt and trousers. My cousin would sing, *'Tinopal, Tinopal......'* an advertisement for a brand of indigo, which, it was claimed, brought extra shine and whiteness to the clothes. Occasionally, Manik's mother came to our place in the evenings, after finishing with her daily work, and would have tea and *paan* together with my grandmother and my aunt. My grandmother was an old woman, slight in built and short. She got her hair cropped so that it was more manageable. Being of a short stature, she placed a stool below her foot for support. The women would sit together and chat for some time. One day Manik's mother had a proposal.

'What if I marry my son to your granddaughter?'

My grandmother couldn't have asked for anything more.

So Somya and my cousin were now in the same family. My grandmother knew Somya too, being neighbours. When we were children and at school, one of the peons would come and take me to the principal's room. I would be scared; has someone complained against me? It was with a sense of relief that I saw *Pujama*, my grandmother, and my aunt, sitting there, the bloody *paan* juice tracing its path on the older woman's furrowed chin, chatting with Somya's mother, the school principal. My grandmother would take a walk up to the school after breakfast, at least once a fortnight, and she straightaway headed towards the principal's room. And Somya's mother, in true neighbourly spirit, would ask her to be seated in her room, while a peon would be sent to fetch me.

Restlessness is something that always characterized Somya. When in school, she would fling shoes at her mother when she wanted to go out and was stopped from doing so. She did not like any kind of restrictions on herself, least of all, from her mother. When a child, she told her mother, 'I want to pee in your *saree*.' She got a few slaps from her mother, who, later on, locked her in the bathroom. Somya kept wailing, kicking at the door, throwing the bar of soap in the plastic bucket, half full, kept below the tap. All this elicited no response from her mother. She found her uncle's new checked shirt, with a breast pocket and half sleeves. She dipped her face in water in the bucket, that had now become white with all the soap dissolving, and then she scrubbed her face with her uncle's shirt. When her uncle went to the bathroom after the door was unbolted and she was freed, he was astonished to see his new shirt, soaked in water. 'Who did this?' he shouted, holding the wet shirt between two fingers, a towel wrapped on his torso. Somya's mother knew who had been to the bathroom, and before Somya could escape to her room, her uncle caught hold of her and slapped her on her face. She sat in a corner, weeping, when her father entered, and took her on his lap. 'No one loves me, no one loves me,' she wiped her nose in her father's shirt.

'No, but I love you,' he said, and Somya bit him in his stomach. He did not raise a finger.

When Somya died, it was her mother who wept incessantly. She has quit the school and now devotes her time in taking care of Somya's second child. Somya had died while giving birth to this child. When I went to Somya's house to offer my condolences, I was surprised to see her father, discussing Somya's death in the same vein he had talked to me about the elections. No emotions, no suffering. Those who had come to offer condolences sat silently, staring at Somya's corpse, flies hovering on her face, her lips parted. It seemed she smiled at the world that tried to fetter her hands at every step. Somya always did what she wanted to; she left the world with no unfulfilled desire, no dreams shattered.

All the family members and some others went to the *Baans Ghat* for Somya's cremation. Her uncle also went there, wearing the same kind of shirt Somya had wet as a child. When *ghee* was poured, the wood crackled, her flesh burned. They all stood there, watching, until there remained nothing but a heap of ash and a few bones. Somya's uncle then remarked bitterly, 'we have burnt the sinner,' and walked away.

My Friend Sheena

I had a friend, Sheena. She was not great looking. Neither did she have the beautiful smile that wins you over. Sheena was tall, tall for her age, her hair falling all over her forehead. She had the confidence none of us in the class had.

Mrs. M was our class teacher. One who did not like the parents peeping into the classroom to get a glimpse of their children, sitting there for the first time, their faces serious, frightened and confused. My seat was in the corner, my name pasted on the chair that was allotted to me. Mrs. M drove all the parents, over anxious, away from the window; she said it was not a zoo, the children should be left to her care.

It was Sheena who came to me. I didn't go to her. My mother had given me a doll which I kept in my bag. I would look at it occasionally for some comfort. Sheena saw the doll. She came to me, smiled, and held my hand.

I liked seeing Mrs. M early in the morning, her hair wet, wearing bright lipstick, the shades changing every day. Now that was one thing I didn't like about Mrs. M and told *Ma* about it.

'Look, *Ma,* is this fair? Look at ma'am. She changes her dress everyday and asks us to wear the same shirt with same pinafore, the name of the school written on it! And she changes the colour of her lipstick everyday!'

Sheena had a friend, Shefalika. The tall, bony girl, suffered from polio; this made her sit out practically from all the sports classes. She was the lucky one, who sat under the tree and watched us play, with her hair getting covered with flowers, reddish yellow in colour.

Sheena and Shefalika talked of things like boys and Shakespeare in later years. Shefalika, the great *rattoo,* who mugged up everything. She had all the speeches of 'Merchant of Venice' by heart and talked of things like goblin, goblet and gondola. I said, 'Look Sheena, why doesn't your friend go with a goblin on a gondola to a place where she can drink from a goblet?' Unimpressed by my eloquent speech, Sheena remained her friend.

Mrs. M, of those early years, had some fascination for *chappals,* especially those which had two straps. She made us draw *chappals* in black pencil which we were asked to colour with crayons, those short thick colour pencils which I loved rubbing against the white sheet Mrs. M provided us. We were then asked to hang them in class.

We had a *dosawallah* in school. He turned out crisp *dosas,* filled with potatoes, mashed and fried in red hot chillies and onion. He then served them in plates made of leaves. Then he put some *chutney* in the corner of the plate which we grabbed. Shefalika waited for her turn.

'Sheena, you know, Shakespeare never ate *dosas,*' I made an observation, addressing Sheena and looking at Shefalika.

It was Mrs. B's farewell. She was our chemistry teacher. We sang sad songs for her, she cried for us. Everyone cried along with her. Sheena and I. Those who could not cry, however much they tried, tried recollecting sad moments of their lives so that they could produce at least some tears, they wanted to display they were not less sensitive.

I met Mrs. B a few days back on Janpath, the same old Mrs. B. She enquired about Sheena and I told her. She didn't say anything, simply looked at me, her grey eyes moist.

'She was a very close friend of yours, wasn't she?'

'Yes.'

'God and his ways!' she walked away, her *saree* dusting the streets of Janpath, the shopping bags in her hands, stuffed with clothes she had bought for her grandchildren. *Dussehra* was near.

We passed out from school. Childhood friendship ensured that Sheena and I got ourselves enrolled in the same college. The seats in hostel were scarce, we rented out a room at rupees one thousand per month, exclusive of water and electricity charges. Heater we were not supposed to use. In fact, it was fun to see the speed with which the meter ran when we used the heater, without informing the landlord. I stood guard while Sheena prepared tea or coffee. Another thing forbidden in that house was non-vegetarian food. We told the landlord we were brahmins, who normally don't eat meat, and then entered into a contract with the caterer- one of those smart types who sent *rotis* wrapped in silver foil, with some *saunff* and sugar packed in small polybags, the size of a child's palm. He provided chicken on Fridays and fish on Saturdays. The boy who delivered the food at our place came exactly at nine, the bicycle bar loaded with packets of food, *tin tin tin.* Now this *tin tin tin* served dual purpose. The boy derived some entertainment by this *tin tin tin.* It also gave us notice so that we stood at the gate, snatching the packet from the boy and running upstairs, taking care that the landlord never came to know what we ate especially on Fridays and Saturdays.

We remembered each day by what the caterer gave us to eat, for example, we had chicken day, fish day or the detestable *tinda* day. On chicken days a single piece of chicken floated in pale orange gravy. I had the gravy and Sheena the chicken piece. On days when we received fish, normally a large head, its eyes gorged out, its mouth open, smiling, it was my turn to have the large head. So while the smiling fish, its eyes missing, continued to smile in my stomach, Sheena ate her *rotis* with the gravy and the salad consisting of onion and cucumber.

Sheena was the tall one. The mature one. When in school, she played the mother and I the baby. The baby with four missing teeth. The teeth that had been knocked off when I was climbing on the monkey bar, then hanging, I lost my grip, fell head on.

I was sad when I heard Sheena couldn't have a baby. She wanted a baby more than I did.

She was the one who got married first. I heard her husband beat her at times. She bore it with fortitude. Sheena, the ambitious one, said she wanted to work as an airhostess. Her husband said she did not need wash the dirt of strangers.

'Remain a maid at home,' he said, 'why outside?'

She came to know of everything by and by. Sheena's husband wanted to marry a woman he had worked with. The leech. He was angry with his parents, decided to marry Sheena, and then went to the local doctor to get himself sterilized. Sheena's married life was a hell, especially the first few years. While her husband slept with that woman, Sheena prepared delicacies for them, served them, and then heard them laugh over a silly joke the woman cracked now and then.

The woman left him four years after their marriage. She got interested in a man working in the US, in the IT sector, a big man, drawing a fat salary. Sheena's husband was left behind to feel his smallness.

Sheena adopted a baby.

She gave him a nice massage early in the morning, with mustard oil she got in a bowl, the baby gurgled. The baby lay on his back, doing 'aaaaaa', sucking his thumb, trying to eat the end of Sheena's *saree*. Then she heated some water, filled the baby's tub with it, and then very gently, she lowered the baby in water. While she used one hand to hold the baby's head, a soft ball with tufts of hair on it, with the other she splashed water on his face. The baby laughed. Then she wrapped him in a soft towel, wiping his face very carefully, sprinkled talcum powder on his body, applied some cream on his face, and then dressed him up. The baby was asleep by then. Then she would lay him on his mattress, and cover him with a small sheet. The baby slept like an angel, his hands spread out.

Then she would boil the bottles. In a large vessel she would put all the bottles, the nipples detached, and let water simmer for some time. She would wipe them with a clean piece of cloth, pile them up in a small tub and then arrange them neatly. Those days were hectic but Sheena loved doing all that and would say, the baby on her lap, the bib fastened to his neck while she would feed him,

'When you grow up, and I stoop with age, won't you look after me?' The baby would grunt in response, hardly aware of his responsibility.

Sheena's husband never really liked the child. But somehow, somewhere he was developing this soft corner for Sheena. Once he got a *kanjeevaram* for her, flaming red, Sheena smiled, 'red, flaming red, at this age?' This infuriated her husband, he pushed her out of the door and said she had to spend the night on the bench in the park, flaming red or no flaming red. She kept scraping at the door, pleading, yet not very loudly for she didn't want the neighbours to wake up and see. The baby was terrified, sensitive creature; he was flung onto her lap. Both were shivering, no shawl, no woollens. It was chilling, the cold wind stabbing at their flesh. Sheena walked towards the adjoining park, crouched under the bench, sparkling white, its surface gleaming in soft moonlight. The trees stood there, protecting Sheena from prying eyes, its branches drooping, looking at her with kind eyes. The blades of grass swayed occasionally when cold wind blew, Sheena held the child closer to herself. She didn't know when she fell asleep. When she woke her up the following morning, still dark, the child was already dead.

The child was wrapped up in a white piece of cloth and lowered into a small hole in the ground. She started life anew.

I heard she had obtained a divorce. It was all very smooth and both parties were relieved. Sheena started working as a newsreader on television, she entered into a relationship with a fellow newsreader.

It was her grit and determination, which helped Sheena overcome the hurdles in life. Husband-less, childless Sheena, never lost faith in herself. When I saw her on TV, I made enquiries. Yes, it was my Sheena. I went to her studio one day, met her while she was emerging from it, I took her to a restaurant where we sipped coffee and discussed things like children, and life.

She did not have a child but she did have life.

Sheena had now started staying with an old lady. Very fat, with silver hair neatly parted in middle, and wearing *pyjamas* that were loose, Sheena's landlady cooked for her, including lunch and dinner, prepared her bed, and gave her company on days when Sheena did not need to go for her work. In return, she had to shell out two thousand rupees per month. Sheena would smile when she saw her landlady's love for money. But who doesn't love money? At times Sheena would be horrified to find herself patting her leather purse, with currency notes, on her pay day. Very proud, she would go to the grocer's, clear the bills, buy a glass of orange juice, served in thick, long glasses, gulping it quickly, and then head for a movie theatre to see the latest movie.

Life really did not come to an end for Sheena. No marriage this time. It was a live-in relationship. Very modern, considering the society Sheena lived in. Sheena shifted to her new apartment, a two-bedroom accommodation, with balconies attached to the rooms. They hardly had any furniture. Sheena loved living in a house which was decorated and had plenty of furniture, filled with modern gadgets. On pay day, Sheena would take half a day off, visit all the good showrooms, and buy one thing after another. At times she would shell out hard cash, and some other time use the credit card, signing wherever she was asked to, issuing post-dated cheques, promising to pay the balance in equal instalments. Like the bird trying to rebuild her nest, Sheena started collecting things, one by one. Her new man was not bad at heart, he did not beat her or something, but he was one of those who believed life was one big party. Nothing beyond that. So while Sheena slogged, almost tired to death, her live-in partner sat at home and blew Sheena's money. Sheena's hard earned money. And Sheena hated it. So she told him.

'Start working and for heaven's sake, help me,' her voice quivering, Sheena was desperately trying to steady her voice, she never liked others see her cry.

Manish understood but he couldn't help it. And how could he? He was almost half Sheena's age, his friends were still in college.

I met Mrs. M. The one who had this fascination for *chappals* which had two straps. Sheena liked Mrs. M. Mrs. M was one of those who would teach you that you need to brush twice daily, would compel you to do 'eeeee', bare your teeth which she would then inspect and give you a pass mark if she felt they were clean enough. And Mrs. M was organized. When we were asked to keep our worksheets and crayons in the pigeon hole, it was Sheena who impressed Mrs. M with her orderliness. All her worksheets were neatly folded, kept in the folder she was given most meticulously, and it was Sheena, the only one in the class, who managed to keep all her crayons with their sharpened end facing upward. All others were disorganized. Some crayons pointed this way and some that way.

Mrs. M never liked Sheena for her live-in relationship.

'Why don't you marry him?' Mrs. M asked.

'Not again,' Sheena shuddered, marriage to her was nothing but blows and abuses.

'You can't have the same kind of experience every time,' Mrs. M was trying to convince, to cajole her.

Mrs. M called me up one day. Sheena had been my friend, my close confidante. I had some influence over her. Why didn't I try to convince her? Did I really have any influence over Sheena? I was wondering. I, who couldn't keep away Sheena from Shefalika, the latter I hated and the former I loved. All my statements on Shefalika and Shefalika's Shakespeare did not influence Sheena much. What I couldn't do then, how could I do now?

But Mrs. M saw to it that I visited Sheena regularly. Most of the time Sheena would not be at home, it was Manish who gave me company. I would find him in their main balcony, a cigarette on his lips, standing up to say 'hi' when he saw me standing below. We talked of weather and books and the advantages of marriage. He said he didn't have any problem. Sheena was his love, why didn't I talk to Sheena about it? About other things I could talk to him. In fact, he loved talking to me, he told me. My kind of face fascinated him.

I told Mrs. M I was not going there again. Mrs. M said I had to meet Sheena in private and I had to tell her. But what do I tell her? About the fascination that Manish had for my kind of face? I didn't tell Sheena nor did I tell Mrs. M about it. Instead, I asked Sheena,

'How is Shefalika? Does she still talk of Shakespeare?'

Sheena smiled. 'You have not grown up,' she remarked.

I visited their house again and again, goaded by Mrs. M, talked about Shefalika and Shakespeare.

'Have some milk at night before going off to sleep,' I suggested, her haggard looks I didn't like at all.

'And cut down on tea and coffee that you keep having all day.'

'Shefalika would have said the same thing.'

This time she smiled. 'You will never change. Who would say you are married with two children?'

I knew I was married. Married women fascinated him. The man was telling me. Why didn't Sheena see what I saw? Like a slave she worked for him, served him. In return, he didn't beat her. That was all. His responsibility was over.

'Look here,' I asked her one day, 'what kind of future do you have?'

'Why?' she asked, munching *tilkut* her mother had sent.

She obviously failed to see what I saw.

But I was not prepared for this. Sheena, why did you do it? Sheena, you knew. Sheena you had known it all along.

She had not tried to dodge the police. She knew the arms of law were long.

Mrs. M paid her a visit. 'You were my brightest student,' she looked at Sheena's nails, overgrown, 'I had thought you will make me proud of you.' She had got a pair of *chappals* for Sheena. A gift for her favourite student.

Her ex-husband came to see her in the cell. 'You've grown old,' she remarked, giving him a feeble smile.

'Did you marry again?'

He gave her a long, deep look.

And then he said, 'no.'

Life is strange. He was sounding distant. While you were with me, I hated you. At times I wanted to kill you. Instead, it is you, the docile one, who has killed a man. I thought you couldn't hurt a fly. Didn't your hands shake?

'I'm tired,' she said in response.

I also went to see her.

'Shall we talk of Shefalika and Shakespeare?' her eyes were smiling. I wondered what she looked like when she saw him prostrate before her, the vanquished one, thick blood streaming out of his stomach, dirtying her rug, the rug that she had bought.

'Sheena,' my voice was at a very low pitch, my hands were shaking as I held her.

Her expressions changed and she said, 'I am tired. Very tired.'

'You know what', she was saying, 'you think I didn't know Manish? Didn't I know you wanted to tell me about him while all you did was talk about Shefalika and Shakespeare? Poor man. He looked so serene, lying there, his eyes bulging out, as if he were seeking an explanation from me. I did not even wash my hands. He had a long way to go. Only I didn't let him. I was tired. I was battered by my ex-husband, I didn't do anything, the baby died, the baby I had nurtured and loved, the baby who died while we lay crouched under that white bench. I should have killed my ex-husband then. I didn't. Instead I killed him. He was only a boy. Slightly playful, careless. But I think it is my tiredness which did it.' It was easy to talk of Shefalika and Shakespeare. It didn't tire her.

And then Sheena wept, she didn't try to hide her tears. No Sheena, I was telling her, you need not be smart and confident. It seems the tables have turned. But we didn't mind.

No longer the smart Sheena, the confident one. But Sheena who is tired. She got up after some time, wiped her face with the end of *saree* and then gave me a bright smile.

'Shefalika come to see me yesterday,' she had a naughty look on her face.

Blue Shorts And T-Shirt

His mother was not happy. Her son had cleared the Combined Defence Services examinations. Mr. Pandit, her husband, a tall and wiry man, was however, proud. He thought of his son, medals on his chest, arranged in a row.

They had called him Captain Anurag Pandit- a tall man, and very fair. His father's height and mother's complexion, a perfect blend, they said. His college friends suggested he should go for modelling, he had the poise, the presence. But Anurag knew he would join the army. When he was a child, he remembered he would get excited when he heard patriotic songs, aired on All India Radio. Shantanu, his friend, now an executive with a US multinational, often said, 'Who knows, Anurag, you may have been Subhash Chandra Bose in your previous life.'

'Shantanu,' he asked, 'what if I do not make it?'

Shantanu laughed. 'In that case,' he smiled, white teeth flashing, 'I will resign, and we will start our own firm.'

He had passed the test. His mother, while pressing his clothes, thought of him. She couldn't bear to send him away, but there he was, bathed, his hair neatly combed, polishing his shoes, dark brown. She looked at him.

'Ma, I will not drink too much,' he had promised, searching for approval in his mother's eyes.

'Keep writing,' she had said, a slight tremor in her voice. He got up, put an arm across her shoulders, and whispered, 'Anurag Pandit can not march onward unless his mother gives the orders.'

Colonel uncle, Shantanu's father, had come in the evening. They had celebrated with Seagram's Hundred Pipers. Colonel uncle was reminiscent of the war days of 1971, when he had won battle after battle, his *jawans* spitting fire, decimating anything that came in the way.

'Anurag', Shantanu's sister, Mira, had said, 'my brother will miss you.'

He recalled the day Colonel uncle had come to stay in their colony, Patliputra. The bed made of cane, the circular dining table, the six chairs, polished and upholstered, the mattress belonging to their son, which had big images of joker printed on it, they had all come loaded on the truck.

Shantanu and he had played cricket together. Shantanu bowled and he batted. Almost always he had won but Shantanu, a spirited man, did offer a stiff resistance. They grew up together eyeing the girls of the colony, chasing the rickshaws with *chicks* on their bicycles. His sister had been a doll. Sweet and chirpy, she insisted she played with them, he never really minded it. In fact he had loved playing badminton with her, secretly admiring her. But Shantanu was very short tempered, right from the beginning. They often quarrelled while playing. Once Shantanu had flung him in a *nullah,* after a heated argument. While he lay prostrated, Shantanu stood there, abusing him. Then

Shantanu jumped into the *nullah*, caught hold of him by his collar, pulling him up.

He smiled as he remembered all this. He looked at Mira.

'Won't you miss me?'

She had remained quiet, her face blank.

'I will ring up when I reach there,' he had said quietly.

The ambassador car, frog-like, painted black and yellow, pulled up before their house. With the help of the driver, they had loaded his suitcases. The car moved, they all stood there, waving. Mrs. Pandit sighed.

Several years had passed. He had come home on a vacation. Soon he had received orders to get back.

Kargil was in news. The counter offensive by India was imminent. Captain Anurag Pandit was to lead one such offensive.

Mira would often come to their house, to meet his mother, on some pretext or the other. Often there was no excuse.

'Auntie, shall I make tea for you?' Mira asked.

His mother nodded. They sat before the TV, sipping tea silently.

'Anurag's letter,' his mother said, hardly audible, pushing the white envelope towards Mira.

She held it, her lips moving, as she read. She felt relieved.

'So now he is Captain Anurag Pandit.'

His father walked in. 'Anurag has tremendous responsibilities,' he beamed at his wife, 'still he finds time to write to us.'

'He loved playing cricket,' his mother remarked, 'and he always wanted to join the army.'

When a child, he had stuck to Colonel uncle, like the lice on the scalp. 'Anurag!' Colonel uncle had called him to his room one day, and had said, smiling, 'Why don't you stop playing cricket in my backyard?' He suggested a better site, and to make the idea appealing, Colonel uncle went with them, to a deserted piece of land. He was quite enthusiastic. 'Uncle will be in my team !' he announced. 'Yes son!' Colonel uncle said. The old man had played with them for a while after which he went away.

'He was your father's fan,' his mother told Mira.

Mira had gone to his house again, after ten days.

They were quiet. Mira was feeling uncomfortable.

'You don't look well Mira,' his mother rose, saying so she started piling cushions, one on top of the other, 'lie down on this couch.'

Mira could smell him, the smell of his cologne wafting.

'I want some water,' Mira ran to the kitchen, something was terribly wrong.

Mira had loved him, she knew. Was she losing her head? She pulled open the refrigerator, selected a chilled bottle, and drank water in gulps.

Mira's hands were shaking. She had difficulty in holding the bottle. She could feel him all over the place. She staggered. She pulled at the lace tablecloth, the vase fell, spilling water.

There was a letter. Mira made an effort to open her eyes, she could see a boy sitting on the floor, next door, all his crayons spilled out of the red oblong bag, with loops made of satin, his face full of concentration. The boy's sister sat silently next to him, picked up a crayon, and began outlining a flower.

His mother looked at Mira. She gave the letter to her, unopened. Mrs. Pandit looked out of the window. Her eyes were fixed on a bird, drinking water, its neck bent. She watched the bird. It drank water, and it flew.

'Anurag is injured,' Mira said, 'he is in the army hospital.'

His mother continued to look out of the window. A boy, wearing blue shorts and yellow T-shirt, was cycling on the deserted road. Suddenly he was on the ground, his face contorted. Mrs. Pandit knew he was about to cry. She remembered her son.

'Auntie,' Mira whispered, 'Anurag has done us proud. He has fought valiantly.' His mother said nothing. She could see the boy in blue shorts and yellow T-shirt get up; he dragged himself towards the bicycle, its yellow basket covered with dust.

Her son was stubborn, Mrs. Pandit knew. When a child, he had once refused to take bath. He wore his school dress, tied his shoelaces, and was about to take the water bottle when she had seen him.

'Did you take bath?' she had enquired.

'No,' he was defiant, 'yesterday I had taken bath, today I will not.'

In a fit of rage, she had dragged her son, and put him under the shower, fully dressed. He had wailed, drenched in water. But he usually had his way, she knew. She never wanted her son to join the army but he had not listened to her. 'Don't hold his hand,' her husband would scold her, 'give Anurag his freedom.' She had given him his freedom. And there he was, lying in a hospital, hundreds of miles away.

There was a knock. Mira opened the door, her father stood on the doorway. 'Hurry up Mira, our neighbour, Major Pratyush Sharma, has been killed.' Mrs. Pandit stood up. *'Bhai saab,* I will come with you', she said.

Pratyush's mother, her head covered with a white *dupatta,* was sitting on the floor, surrounded by ten to fifteen people. They were all silent. She looked at her younger son, who sat next to her. 'Today he shall take the test his brother had taken,' she said.

'I want him to join the army,' Pratyush's mother continued, a determined look on her face.

Anurag's mother got up after ten minutes. On her way, she saw the boy in blue shorts and yellow T-shirt. She looked at him fondly. He was talking to his mother, holding her hands.